Female: 918

By
Jason Ellis

Exist.
Survive.
Live.

Female: 918
PART I: EXIST & SURVIVE

PAPERBACK EDITION
Published by Jason Ellis/ JTT Publishing.

Page nine illustration by Sharon Stone. Copyright © 2014 Sharon Stone.
www.facebook.com/SharonStoneArtpage

Cover design: Kylie Gray. Copyright © 2016

PAPERBACK EDITION ISBN 13: 978-1-906529-91-8
KINDLE EDITION ISBN: 978-1-906529-90-1

JTT Publishing books may be ordered through all internet booksellers, or through your local book retailer.

Dedications

As always, for my family.
For my friends.
For the readers.

Prologue

Complete darkness surrounds my body. This is a place where light is forbidden, even unwilling and scared, to enter.

Every attempt I make at movement feels constricted, like I am swimming, or trying to, through thick oil. I feel heavy, my body is covered. Every breath I draw in carries a bitter flavour, and the air is laced with a corrosive mix of heat and fear. It is intimate, personal, one I can recognise without hesitation.

Am I alone here? I think. I wait for an answer from my own mind, yet silence lingers.

I can feel something ... someone ...

I sense another soul swimming with me. They are different to me, unhindered. Yes, they can move through the oil with ease. Their soul is somehow connected to this place, as if the same heart beats for them both.

Who are you? Where are you?

For whatever reason, I do not have an audible voice here. My words are stolen by the darkness, swallowed back up as quickly as they are produced.

The odour of salt and sweat swims side by side with the oil. If I let it in, if I let it pour down to my lungs, I know it will scrape at them from the inside and invade my body.

"Take aim!" A female voice, acidic and dominant, slices through the murky depths. The thick oil is split by the words, as if they are a sharp sword. I know the one wielding this weapon.

That voice ... no ... you can't be here with me, that is impossible! You can't hurt me ... I am not afraid ...

"… And …" A deliberate pause follows. It *always* follows. The feeling of power and the exhilaration it offers has to be extended and savoured. The moment between life and death is one of ultimate and infinite possibilities: a millisecond in time, a lifetime of memories, a wide universe or a grain of sand. They all exist equally, waiting for their chance to stand at the forefront, waiting to be chosen as the final thought.

This place is changing. Somehow, I am now able to see through the pungent gloom that clings to my skin. In front of me there are …

NO! How am I able see them? I don't understand any of this!

I am suddenly confronted with a line of grey and terrified faces and I wish for the complete darkness to blind me again. A mixture of eleven people stand in total: male and female, teenagers through to the elderly.

I recognise all of you ... Glimpses of my early life, brought back to haunt me.

They try to scream as blindfolds appear, yet their voices are stolen just as mine were. The grey rags - dirty, bloodstained, and ripped up in strips - float through the air like leaves on a gentle breeze. They move closer to the people and wrap tightly over their terrified eyes.

"… FIRE!"

••

"NO!" I cry as I sit up in my bed, woken with hateful precision by the nightmare. *I can still taste it! I can taste the oil ... the salt and the sweat!*

My stomach and lower back muscles clench with sharp pulses, as if I have been punched while asleep. I lift my maroon nightshirt a few inches, with care, and massage across the painful areas. I half expect to see bruises crawling underneath my skin.

The early morning sunrise layers through the horizontal slats on the window-blinds and I can see my bedroom glowing with a radiant life. I feel and experience the calm familiarity of the world around me: my clothes are on the floor, as are my black boots, and the furniture is where it has always been.

Do you see that blue top? That pair of jeans? You wore those yesterday ... you took them off last night ... when you were safe. You are still safe now. You are. Believe that.

I'm slowly brought back to the present moment, out of that place, that darkness, away from that ultimate and intoxicating power.

"Just a dream. Just a stupid dream, nothing else," I say in a quiet voice, glad that my words have returned with me from the nightmare.

My eyes, dark-brown, focus on my arm as I watch a bead of sweat trickle down the golden skin for a few seconds. It is the result, the end product, of an exotic mixture of harvested DNA. Apparently, so I have been told over the years, it creates my alluring, Asian elegance.

As I sit, I lose myself completely to the refracted and reflected spectrum inside the miniature drop of liquid. It is so full of colour, so bright. I need it, this timeless contrast. I need the light as my ally. We need to defeat the darkness together.

Loud footsteps thump along the hallway outside of my bedroom.

"Aunt Rain!" Daisy Coast, my seventeen year old adopted niece, cries out as she flings open the bedroom door.

Her blue nightshirt runs a few inches lower on the left

3

shoulder and her blonde hair has obviously been on a pillow very recently - probably less than a minute ago - hence its unkempt style.

Daisy's hazel eyes widen with love and concern as she runs across the room. "Are you okay? I heard you scream! What happened?" She jumps up on the bed and takes my hands in her own.

I force a smile and open my eyes fully. "I'm fine, Daisy … I just need a second to get my head together, that's all," I answer.

"I hate it when you have these dreams." Daisy's teeth clench together.

"Me too." I nod as I free one of my hands from Daisy's tight grip. I run my fingers through my own hair: long, straight, and deep black, like a night sky void of any stars.

"It's been a few months since the last one, at least," Daisy reminds me, attempting to bring a positive to the moment. "They're still less frequent, aren't they? It isn't the same as years ago, when we were younger."

I decline to answer as I sit back on the bed and bring my knees up closer to my chest. Daisy follows, resting on my shoulder.

"I'm sorry that I woke you up, Daisy. What time is it anyway?" I ask.

Daisy turns her head to the right. The projected readout - a flickering and translucent turquoise light - from my mobile communicator hovers in the space above the bedside cabinet. "Ten minutes to six. It's not far off the alarm … so stop worrying. I've told you a million times before that I don't like it when you apologise. You never need to apologise to me, Aunt Rain."

We sit in complete silence for a few minutes, allowing the day to begin. The lack of words does not bring forth a problem, though, for we have a bond, we are two pieces of a whole. Years of peace, trust, and calm silences have passed between us already.

The alarm - with a gentle crescendo - plays birdsong. "Right, six o'clock. Time to get up and check the perimeter," I say.

Daisy nods and sits up first. "I'll go and get dressed," she says as her legs spin around off the edge of the bed.

As I move, a noise, one so quiet I have to question my own sense of hearing, hums from my left forearm. I look down and rub at the skin.

"Is something wrong?" asks Daisy as she swipes her hand over a sensor on the wall. The blinds rise up, stacking themselves neatly at the top of the window with automated movement.

The room floods with more sunlight and growing warmth, pouring in like a waterfall. I move my eyes around for the second time, still taunted by the nightmare. My furniture, inanimate, sparse and boring, helps to ground the troubling thoughts: a wardrobe along the left wall, a dresser opposite the bed, two bedside cabinets, and the burgundy carpet that feels soft under my feet. I can use these everyday objects as anchors. I grab them and hold on when my world crumbles, or I pull myself up the tall ladder back to reality.

"Aunt Rain? Is something the matter?" repeats Daisy. Her voice wavers ever so slightly with growing concern.

I shake my head. "Sometimes it surprises me … my arm … even after all these years. Don't worry yourself. Go and get dressed … and …"

"Yes?"

I turn myself around so that my eyes lock with Daisy's. "Stay with me this morning. We'll walk the fence together," I say, unashamed by the words. I don't want us to split up when carrying out the security checks, as we normally do. I want her by my side. I want her there in case the black oil returns for another attempt to smother and drown me.

Daisy nods. "Of course." She leaves my bedroom as a

smile tries with bravery to form on her lips.

I run my forefinger along my left arm, from the wrist to the elbow. It feels like bone under the skin, even though it is actually a prosthetic creation of metal and wires. I stop at a specific point and push with a little more force. There is a slight dent under my finger, a line of about an inch-and-a-half.

You can't hurt me. You can't. Never again, I think and the darkness clouds across my eyes for a few seconds.

••

Outside our home, both Daisy and I admire the early August morning. Again, we are silent. We don't always need words to communicate with each other.

It doesn't matter to either of us that, in truth, the house we live in isn't anything more elaborate than a two-storey brick cube in the middle of a field. The building and land have always been our very own part of the world since shortly after Daisy's birth. We own a few thousand square feet to live in, at peace, in safety.

The ground slopes with a slight gradient towards the front fence, then, at a much steeper angle, it drops towards the Thames Estuary. This allows us both to view the beach, the sea, and the half-mile wide road and train network that leads out across the water. Somewhere in the distance stands a vast floating city, one of the entrance points to this area, known as Aegis.

"Aunt Rain, are you ready?" asks Daisy. She stands outside the front door of our house with a handgun holstered to the waist of her black trousers. She is also wearing brown boots and a maroon sweater that looks to be tight-fitting.

"Almost," I say and check my right boot. A knife sits inside a leather sheath attached to the side. "Yeah, I'm ready. We'll start by the lake and work our way around. Anti-clockwise today. Never get set in a routine, Daisy, always remember that. You never kn ..."

Daisy jumps in and finishes the sentence for me. "Know if you are being watched. Routines give them a chance to learn, or discover, a weakness."

I swing an automatic rifle over my shoulder, roll up the sleeves of my beige top, then check the back pocket of my jeans, feeling the mobile communicator inside. "Good girl. Shame you don't listen to me with that kind of enthusiasm when I ask you to clean up your bedroom," I say with a dry tone.

Daisy rolls her eyes and smiles as she starts to walk across the short grass towards the perimeter fence. Even though she can't see my face, she knows it carries exactly the same expression.

Daisy and I arrive by the lake a few minutes later. It is an imperfect circle with an approximate diameter of three-hundred feet. I do swim here, just ... not very often. It's too painful ... emotionally painful.

Although we are here for more important reasons, we both stand for a few moments, mesmerised by the tiny flecks of morning sunlight catching the surface of the water. They dance from place to place and glide across the ripples.

Daisy walks away and checks the fence. "Green lights here, Aunt Rain."

"Same here." I nod my head after doing the same.

The border of our property is completely surrounded with electrified movement detectors - poles of steel alloy that stand eight feet high. They are all fitted with an array of sensors running from ground level.

I wait for Daisy to walk the ten or so strides between the poles and join me. "I'm sure I just saw a few fish by the surface. I should really get down here more often," I say.

Daisy takes my hand in a gentle grip. "I'd love that," she says. "It's one of my favourite places to sit and read, draw ... listen to music. I'm meeting with Sky and Jay down here later this morning."

My memory sparks, in a positive manner, as Daisy mentions the names of her friends. I travel back in time for a moment and see their parents standing beside me.

"You're lucky, Daisy, as I was at your age, to have such close friends," I say as some of the events from my past flow through me. "Sky has learnt a lot from her mother ... so courageous and intelligent." The images continues through my mind, playing out the amazing and tragic, the love and grief. They stop at Jay's father, *River,* and an unexpected kiss.

I roll my eyes and smile widely. "Keep your eye on Jay. He's a handsome young man ... and *too much* like his father at that age!"

Daisy laughs. "I've heard these stories before ... and you always stop at the good parts!" she says, willing me to add more details.

Despite the jovial conversation, my serious attitude returns without warning. It's always with me, I can never escape from it. "I know it's an amazing place, Daisy. It's ... difficult, that's all. You see beauty, I see something ... something very different."

Another memory sparks which does not cause a smile. Instead, it causes my heart to thump hard in my chest and my stomach to tighten. "And ... you know why," I say as my eyes scan across the water.

Daisy looks across the small lake, as I do, back towards the house. I can read her face. I know she is trying to imagine the scenes that I have described to her over the years. How can she, though? How can she imagine them? Bombs exploding all around me, bodies scattered on the floor ... blood and screams everywhere. At least twenty died in the crater that would become this lake. I remember that morning. It's burnt inside my eyes for the rest of my life. An impulsive memorial, built and reinforced by hundreds of hands in a matter of hours. I have every right to see a different side to it - my own tears flow without guilt in this lake, my sorrow swims unseen through the water.

"Let's keep moving." I walk off, sober in thought, heading up the slope to the back of the property.

Almost ten minutes later, we reach the second corner and check the sensors. Each step forward is a small reassurance of safety, easing my fears. I know they aren't warranted after so many years, I honestly do. I can't escape my past, though, and I know that. It has moulded my present self and become a part of me … a part of my personality, my inner self.

My shoulders are low, I take slower steps near this part of the field, and my muscles tense up.

"Are you going in this morning?" asks Daisy.

I don't need to answer my niece's question with words because my body language speaks for me instead. Only years of practise and control manage to stop me from screaming out a reply.

A section of the grass here has been clearly marked with a line of stones, just three or four high - the most basic of walls. It doesn't fit with the whole scene, though, and looks out of place, even out of time. Rustic and hand-crafted skills sit next to the present day technology of the motion sensors. I want it to stand out. I want it to be different, to draw attention. People should stop here and give a few moments of their time to stare, to learn the story.

"Maybe later." I mumble my answer.

Two rusted platforms - large discs which moved and spun around at one point in my past - mark the entrance. Time has covered them in grass and sprinkled tiny wild flowers all over, like natural guardians, rising to protect those lain for years behind them.

I flick a glance at the larger stones inside, some with flowers near to them: bellflower, fuchsia, dahlia. A wild and random blend of colours and aromas.

There are words - some unusual - scratched and painted on the stones: Ocean, Leaf, Blossom … Loudmouth, Gappy, Tick-Tock. I remember every letter. Some are by my hand, some by others.

I pause as my eyes force another look. I have no choice but to submit and give myself permission to smile, despite the mental pain. I can't deny or smother the conflicting memories.

Daisy is watching me as I stand by the cemetery. I can feel her eyes on me, wishing me to feel anything except sadness. She will wait until this moment has passed, with silence and respect. It is now a routine for her, as much as this is for me, one that she has learnt during her upbringing. I'm proud of her, I hope she knows that. So very, very, proud.

I brush my hand through the grass on one of the rusted platforms and the edges of my lips twitch. I can hear them crying out from the past. I can hear the gun turrets that lived here. They screamed in such a unique way, such a stuttered and shrill voice as the bullets flew out.

My eyes turn hazy, glistening with the promise of a tear. *You lost. I planted many of these flowers ... I carried the stones ... as did my friends. I told you there could be a different world, a different way of life! I see these flowers grow throughout the year ... smothering the skeletons of these weapons with their ... their power to live and survive! These ... these machines of death. They will never harm again ...*

Wait! What's that? I hear a noise. It's soft, quite close, and it shouldn't be near me.

With a sudden skill, one that I have mastered through necessity, my feet and hips move and shift to a firm stance.

I lock my body in position.

I am a stone statue.

I am immovable.

Listen. Ignore all that should be here. Focus only on that which does not belong.

The automatic rifle arcs off of my shoulder, like a part of my body, my wing preparing for flight. I hear it cut the air and feel the strap moving over me. It feels perfect ...

natural, exactly as it should. My hands raise and the rifle lands in my tight grasp. A violent ballet move, performed without error.

My eyes dance left and right. I point the barrel just beyond the perimeter fence and peer through the scope.

Listen ...

I push my finger on the trigger in preparation to fire. My nostrils flare as I control my heart rate and breathing.

Out of the corner of my eye, I can see that Daisy has raised her own weapon. Another reason I am so proud of her. I know what it feels like to be protected by friends, by those you love and trust, and I know the responsibility of being the protector, too. It weighs on your shoulders like a boulder that you want to carry, that you are *honoured* to carry.
Daisy has never questioned my advice or training through the years. She mimics my posture, as she has been taught to do, and aims towards the exact same location.

"It's okay, Daisy. It's a deer, that's all. Let's finish up and head back home," I say and allow my muscles to relax. I keep the rifle in my hands for a few more seconds - not unusual behaviour for me in situations like this. I'll fully relax when my senses calm themselves.

"I don't see it, Aunt Rain. Are you sure?" asks Daisy.

The grass beyond the perimeter - the back of the property that belongs to Sky and her family - grows much taller, making it difficult for her to see anything.

"It's there, trust me." I walk away from the cemetery as I speak.

"Where?" Daisy holsters her gun just as the head of a deer bobs up from the grass. She smiles and continues her morning duties.

••

I decide to sit outside the house with a hot drink after my breakfast and a refreshing shower. I will sip my cup of tea, watch birds fly by and listen to their amazing sounds. They soothe me - it's one of the reasons I always wake up to birdsong from my alarm. For many years, too many, I sometimes woke to other sounds: screams, gunfire, and explosions.

There is a patch of the field now covered in flowers, right outside the house. Daisy and I designed it, cultivated the soil, and planted the various seeds. It provides the ideal location for such a morning as this. The colours: green, red, purple, and yellow - in varying tones - bring the area to life somehow, they give it a beautiful voice and presence.

"I'll stay with you today, Aunt Rain, if you want me to?" offers Daisy as she walks out of the house carrying a canvas bag and a sketchbook. She has changed her clothes after the morning security checks and now wears a long and flowing yellow dress. Her hair is neat and tied back with a white ribbon. The warmth of the day, although early still at eight-thirty in the morning, demands she also be barefoot.

I decline with a shake of my head. "Don't be silly, Daisy. I'm fine. If you want to go anywhere else, though, let me know first, that is all I ask of you. Don't go out of sight for too long."

Daisy places the sketchbook in her bag as she walks closer. "I won't, I promise."

She's still unsure about leaving me after the nightmare. I don't blame her in all honesty.

A ladybird lands on my arm and I watch it walk slowly across my skin - the smooth and the scarred. I own healed lines running alone, or intersecting with others, almost forming their own brutal alphabet. I know this language, the one my scars speak. I learnt to speak it fluently years ago, as did many others.

"Go on, Daisy. Meet with your friends and have some fun. It's warm and beautiful out here. I promise I'll join you later … I promise."

Daisy kisses me before walking away in the direction

of the lake.

"It's been beautiful out here for a long time." I whisper more words as the ladybird flies away towards one of the flowers. I smile. Now, at this point in my life, I have so many reasons to.

Part I
Exist and Survive

Chapter one

As sunrise creeps ever closer, the sky creates its own natural and evolving masterpiece. It paints with sweeping strokes and floods colours across the limitless canvas. Blue, purple, and pink stand alone in horizontal drifts, daring to mix with each other, wanting to bring more radiance to the morning, yet waiting patiently for the correct and perfect moment. White clouds - tinted with coral and amber - float at an imperceptible rate, oblivious to their importance in the ceaseless work of art.

A thin sea mist surrounds the anchored city of Europa-Four - one of the thousands built around the world. It is a colossal structure, twenty miles in diameter, housed underneath connected transparent domes. The mist swirls on contact as it begins to crawl up the steel, glass, and thermoplastic in slow drifts, shimmering like a veiled wall of satin.

Waves from the surrounding North Sea lap in a soft rhythm, almost three-hundred feet below the surface. Their gentle ripples are lost, though, overpowered by the usual hum of mechanical and industrial components.

Such an exquisite scene demands attention and many oblige, particularly the enslaved. Those with only broken souls and desolation forcing their hearts to beat, their supply of hope already run dry. They lose themselves, incapable of resistance, needing to feel free and alive as the imminent sunrise plays with their senses. It is majestic and cruel in the same moment.

Three blasts of a klaxon sound, filling the air, covering every inch of the city. Any notion of freedom shatters, as if a bullet - a physical manifestation of suffering and control itself - has been shot through a sheet of glass. The beauty dies at this exact moment, ruined in mere seconds by the sirens, by their significance. *Executions.*

Fear, nausea, shock, and disgust flood through Europa-Four, with dominance and greed directing the waves, steering them so every person is drenched by their force.

A scream shoots through the air - one of the caged and condemned. It only lasts for a couple of seconds yet manages to tell a much larger story to all those it reaches: one of a terrified woman … a woman pleading for forgiveness, for mercy. She knows of the fate which awaits her - she knows, without any doubt, her life will end soon.

Selected panels of the dome darken in rectangular areas as hundreds of concave screens are created in the sky. They are positioned around the perimeter of Europa-Four, measuring four-hundred square feet, to ensure that every person has a view of the upcoming punishments.

The televised brutality will also be broadcast directly to every other screen available in the domain. All eyes need to view it, soak it in, fear it - and fear it completely. Executions will never serve their ultimate purpose if they are not seen and experienced. To witness others being shot - a peer, one that you know, one that shares your despair - the bullets are a powerful and widely employed deterrent, on a global scale.

••

There are seventeen inked dots on the inside of my left forearm - to indicate my age - plus the identifier, *F-918*. That is my name, the only one I have ever been known by. Both the physical alterations are placed there permanently with a chemical procedure. It always stings for a few hours afterwards, the skin raises, and it even bleeds sometimes. The procedure began for me at a young age, though, becoming just another part of my life, an aspect I've endured and adapted to throughout my early years.

In truth, I have no choice but to accept. Like millions of others in the world, I have been created through in vitro fertilisation, then incubated and grown in an amniotic chamber. I am a biological product. I am here solely to serve and toil for others. I do not have any rights, I do not have a name or a voice that can be heard in the world, except my own thoughts, my own internal monologue.

I use mine to drift through Europa-Four, like an invisible entity, unknown to all … free from my physical life. I can stand in the wheat fields of Octant one, sit by the edge of the glinting water used for vast aquaculture hatcheries inside Octant three, or walk amongst fruit bushes and trees in the Octant two orchards. Sometimes, I even climb and sit in the branches, taking in the fictional view around me. My daydreams have evolved to become a method of escape, of finding peace and of subconscious survival.

I always wear a short-sleeve shirt, trousers, and canvas shoes, all in deep burgundy. My body looks naturally thin, bordering on undernourished, and I'm five-four in height. As is standard for females, my black hair has been deliberately cut to only a couple of inches in length. In my imagination, I can change all of that. I can be taller, stronger, or wear different clothes. I choose how I wish to live.

I stand in one of the kitchens that cater for senior military and security personnel, situated in Octant four.

I don't want to see more people die ... why do they force us?

My brown eyes are locked on the smaller screen attached to the wall, despite my loathing for the abhorrent spectacle.

It will be over soon.

The screen is still black as it awaits the live transmission feed. I usually take this opportunity to look at myself in the reflection, to study my face, to see if they have changed me at all, made me age ahead of time. I know of others in their thirties and forties with skin like the cracked leather on the soldiers boots, such is the price of their toil and stress.

Fortunately, I possess a natural beauty which, in my own eyes, still radiates and glows, despite my malnutrition and forced appearance. From the basic geographical education provided in my younger years, I can see that my DNA is of East Asian origin, although I have never been to that part of the world.

There are two security guards standing by the only door to the kitchen, holding automatic rifles. I can see them behind me in the reflection. They always wear black military uniforms, bullet-resistant vests, and helmets. Their unyielding and stern eyes watch the screen with the same intensity as mine do, although they have no reason to fear what is about to happen. I expect there is a sickening enjoyment granted by the immunity and safety they possess.

"Listen up!" shouts the kitchen manager, Darius Marnett. "As soon as the killings are done, you get back to work!" He always speaks with animated hand gestures and lets his muscular body and six-four height pulse superiority throughout the room. He is one of the many people I am scared of.

There are two slaves on early duty this morning as I am here with a younger boy. He is taller than me, five-eight, with blue eyes and blond hair that has been recently shaved to the regulation length of two millimetres. His arms are thin, like mine, like so many others. We both nod with a tense obedience towards Darius.

Are you angry today? Please, don't be angry ...

"I want this floor mopped and the dishes washed. Breakfast for the officers mess is in one hour!"

Darius doesn't need to shout his orders, he carries a menacing appearance with him at all times: cropped brown hair, pumping veins on his neck and face, wide brown eyes shooting a permanent and terrifying gaze, and a square jawline chiselled directly from a slab of rock.

The screen on the wall fades in from black to show the central quad. Ten wooden posts are lined up along a brick wall, ready for their fatal duty, ready to hold their prey in position as the bullets fly through the air.

I don't want to watch this.

The quad is located at the entrance to the administration complex - the entirety of Octant six and seven - which houses all the lavish and extravagant homes on Europa-Four. They belong to the privileged, the rich and powerful, plus, of course, those in control. A quarter of the domain handed over to unimaginable luxury.

A woman in her late-forties, Warden Celestia Horrell - the most important person to reside in Europa-Four - walks across the quad, looking with a cruel admiration at the posts, almost as if she relishes their purpose, their ultimate role in her career and life. She is the person I am most scared of. I fear her with every heartbeat.

Warden Horrell adjusts her military blazer and runs

her hands down any tiny creases in her trousers: both in dark-grey. She glares once more at the posts, kicks one with her black boots to test its firm standing, then climbs a few steps on the side of a raised platform. The assembly of surrounding video cameras zoom in on her location, magnifying and filling all the screens with her tyrannical presence.

Warden Horrell's face always looks unnatural, as if carved out of grey stone, then covered in wrinkled and ashen skin. Deep eyes - that always appeared totally black - stare without mercy, without any spark of emotion. Her wide nose points down and her lips are just a thin, unmoving line. The streaked grey and black hair on her head has been styled with a tight plait this morning. It runs a little lower than her shoulders, like the coiled tail of a scorpion, poised to strike a dose of fatal venom.

"Discipline is key!" she says with a clenched fist. "Without it, there is chaos. Without discipline, we have nothing!"

An uncharacteristic pause follows as Warden Horrell looks around the quad, and further at the outer dome, with tight eyes. She has addressed the half-a-million strong population many times before without the need to reflect, or contemplate her words. "Let this be a reminder to you all that I will not tolerate chaos here!"

The cameras pan and zoom out, adding the row of security guards near the platform to the screen. They salute Warden Horrell and she reciprocates. "Bring them in!" she says in a cold and even tone.

In drilled unison, the guards march away to the holding cell area on the opposite side of the quad. It is an unnecessary display of the regime and all its might. They prove their authority when there is no real need. We are more powerful than you can imagine, fear us.

We do fear you ...

The boy working in the kitchen winces at the screen and his eyes narrow. His head turns with controlled speed and he looks with a sad expression around the kitchen.

Yes, it is disgusting. It is cruel. I feel the same way, I think on seeing his inner pain. Perhaps I should drift away? I could climb a tree in the orchard until the executions are over.

"What?" asks Darius as he wipes two huge hands across his white overalls. "You got something to say to me, boy?"

The boy turns away and chooses to remain silent.

Don't … don't ignore him! Answer him! I make sure my attention is focused on the screen and nowhere else. I'm scared. I have seen what happens to people who annoy Darius.

I can't escape inside my mind, not now!

"What are you staring at?" Darius' voice rises as he speaks the angered words once again. "Hey! Why did you look at me?"

Again, no answer comes. Darius grits his teeth and a vein swells and pulses in his neck. "Don't ignore me!"

The boy turns around again with slow, hesitant, movements and I get to see his identifier for the first time that morning. He has M-532 and sixteen dots inked on his left forearm.

"Yes … sir?" he whispers.

Darius doesn't even bother to speak again. He stomps forward with two long strides and punches the boy in the face with a monstrous fist.

The boy's head snaps back with a sickening crack as he screams in pain and crashes to the floor with blood across his mouth.

Stay calm! Don't react! A jolt of fear fires through my legs and up my spine.

Darius stands over the boy. His nostrils flare and it is obvious he is deciding whether or not to let another punch fly. "You, girl, over here!" he orders.

Me? Please, don't hurt me …

I obey without any thought and move across the

room, forcing myself not to look at the injured boy on the floor. "Yes, sir?" I say.

Darius grabs my arm so that he can see the inked number. "918. You'll be due for fertilization harvesting after the breakfast shift, correct?" he asks.

"I am, sir, yes." I nod and keep my eyes firmly on Darius. I do not want to enrage him even more and fear a harsh slap or a fist might come my way. I've been hit as well, for a lot less, in the past.

Darius nods towards the floor. "Leave now and take him to the hospital with you. Explain to any security that he was punished for insubordination." Darius pauses and only then his fist opens, albeit begrudgingly. "Just ... get him out of my kitchen!"

I allow my eyes to find the boy, M-532. His neck and hands are covered in blood, and there are darker patches on his burgundy shirt as well. He is frozen with terror and pain, still on the floor with a hand pressed against his split lip.

"If anyone need to contact me for an official report, they can." Darius turns back to look at the boy. "Know your place, worthless scum!"

I kneel down and know that Darius can't see my face. I smile as I look at the boy's eyes, saying so much to him without the need for spoken words. *It's over ... he's calmed down ...*

We stand up together and walk towards the security guards by the door. The boy pinches and presses at his lip with blood stained fingers.

"I have to take him to the hospital and report myself in for fertilisation harvesting. Mr Marnett has ordered it," I say to the guards.

Darius, on hearing his surname, turns around and nods his agreement to the security guards. He returns to the screen and the imminent 'killings' straight after. His misaligned judgement has made him care more for the executions than the fact he has just attacked M-532, a boy half his age and physical size.

One of the guards opens the thick steel door and waves his rifle to usher us both outside.

••

A couple of minutes later, once a safe distance away from the kitchen and security mess hall, the boy and I stop walking. We stand next to one of the many train lines that connects Europa-Four with other anchored cities or countries. Thousands of miles of iron and steel are spread across sea and land, like strands on a spider web, linking the globe together. The sun, still rising, lights up half the city while it covers the rest in deep shadows. Tall buildings glow as if made of pure light, just as others strike dark and angry vertical lines. Steel and iron alloys shimmer and hide in obscurity at exactly the same time, unable to exist together in the same space.

The large screens on the dome show Warden Horrell pacing up and down the quad. She checks the chains securing those due to be executed to their posts - another futile exercise with no other purpose than to breed fear. I have worked in the steel mills of Octant four. I know a slave has trouble finding the strength to even lift a heavy chain, let alone break through its metal links.

"What were you thinking? Do you not know about Darius' temper!" I ask. I can't decide if I am upset, furious or concerned for M-532. I can feel my heart beating faster than normal and my eyes are constantly scanning for nearby guards. The whole situation has filled me with a tingling sensation, one that is distressing, one that is too difficult for me to ignore.

The boy lowers his hand and cringes. His lip on the left side is swollen and disfigured - it looks as if he has something in his mouth causing the skin to bulge out. A deep split almost an inch long runs through it, still pumping out blood. "I haven't been here very long. I won't forget, though, trust me. I'll probably have a scar as a constant reminder."

"Where did you transfer from?" I ask as I grab the boy's arm. We start walking again, towards the hospital complex on the outer edge of Octant five. I don't want either of us to be questioned by security guards as to why we are talking with each other on the pathways.

"I spent a little over twelve years in the United Territories. After that, I've been moved around quite a few times." The boy holds his lip again, for a few seconds, and takes some deep breaths in an attempt to ease the stinging sensation. "I've worked in the South and North Atlantic cities, and the Equatorial mainland as well. Before they stuck me in a dark train carriage and brought me here, I cleaned the desalination machines in the climate controlled Arctic regions."

I have only known one place in the world. A part of me wishes to visit other countries and cities, yet I would still see them as a slave, a small cog in the gigantic, uninterrupted, workforce machine. I could be anywhere in the world … any country, territory, floating metropolis, it wouldn't matter, I would always be F-918. I would always be undeserving of a real life.

The boy looks at the large screens on the dome to see an elderly man with a blindfold over his eyes. "He travelled here with me."

I look up and see the elderly man: short and thin with grey hair and a beard. An old scar runs down his right cheek. The chains around his body and neck are causing him pain and cutting at his wrinkled skin.

I want to go … I want to be invisible and float away …

"He isn't guilty of any crime, though. He's just old and slow. A naturally aged body, incapable of working to their quotas. It sickens me!" The boy ignores any physical pain as he spits his angry words out.

I know such corrupted actions are performed on a

regular basis. I remember and old woman who used to be in a cell near to mine: F-368. The system disposed of her in a similar fashion.

She could hardly walk because her legs hurt so much. If you can't walk, you can't work. You can't work hard enough for them ...

"It will change ... one day," says the boy. His words hold an unusual confidence to them, not just a blind hope and need. He looks over his shoulder for a couple of seconds.

I can't see it, even with the power of my imagination. I have tried with all my mental strength to travel and drift through such a world during my life, and I've also permitted myself to dream such absurd thoughts. They never come to me. Even my own imagination - a part of me so personal - seems to be under the control of those in power, banishing any and all optimism from my mind. The vivid daydreams I often create unlock the experience of freedom, yes, but only to a certain degree. They reach a level, an invisible line, a thick wall, and they will not cross it or try to break through.

The boy takes another deep breath as he feels the congealed blood on his split lip, still thick and warm. He watches Warden Horrell on the screens as she returns to the platform. "It's already changing. I've heard stories about it, seen glimpses."

"What?" I ask as my heart jumps towards my throat. "What do you mean?"

"Change! Freedom! It's out there, in so many places."

A dull thump sounds behind us both. Then, a series of sharp and decisive explosions follow.

What was that!?

I hunch forward and raise my hands around my head, forced by instinct to protect myself from the unknown. *That's the kitchen ... and the mess hall!*

My eyes widen as I sink to my knees and pull my arms tighter over my head. The building M-532 and I were working in only minutes before has disappeared ...

obliterated.

The boy stares for a brief moment before he crouches down next to me with what looks to be delayed shock. He doesn't look scared like I am, though.

Why is he acting like this? How can he be so ... calm? Another thought enters my head. *Did he ... he know this was going to happen?*

I listen to the words for a second before deciding they can't be true.

His eyes switch between the explosions - now a rolling fireball filled with chunks of metal - and the elderly man on the screen. "The war started months ago ... They're losing control ... their grip weakens every day ..."

"War?" I hear his words yet I can't comprehend them. It's impossible. *What does he mean? What do your words really mean? Please ... let me understand!*

The boy stares at me, at my troubled face. I have a feeling he can see and even sense the mental fight I am now involved in. He understands because he has a broken and institutionalized mind, as I do.

Can he travel further? Can he walk in a future that is ... free? Why can't I?

A loud klaxon bellows through Europa-Four as the screens zoom to Warden Horrell's face once again. A security guard stands near her, passing on details of the incident. Her black eyes squint, lips purse, and the creases on her brow increase in number. She points to the side of the raised platform and speaks quietly - still through gritted teeth - to a man with a computer tablet in his hands. He nods and the screens black out, ending their domain wide transmissions with a sudden accuracy.

I hear the rhythmic thud of military boots as a platoon of soldiers hurtle towards us both on their way to secure the area.

The boy stares at me again. Despite his injured lip, he manages a smile and his eyes widen, glistening with the reflected sun and thick flames. "… And we're going to win," he says.

Chapter two

The unexpected and violent explosions set off a chain reaction of events, sweeping through Europa-Four like a tornado of decisive precision. The city itself becomes like a machine which has been switched on by an unseen hand, one connected to the flames and smoke. It is suddenly whirring and grinding, churning out calculations to produce movements and actions.

More platoons and companies from the military arrive and position themselves in various locations, the doors on buildings are sealed closed, and metal shutters roll down over windows. Every person not connected to the military or security divisions vanishes from the pathways. They are either ordered to by the swarming soldiers, or it is an act of their own self preservation.

What's happening?

My eyes set their gaze on the remains of the mess hall and kitchen building once again. Smoke and flames still rage with relentless fury. A concoction of spraying lines of fire and rolling mushrooms of grey and orange churn skyward.

Darius ... and the guards? They couldn't have survived that!

As my hands shake and sweat forms on the back of

my neck, I remember the words the boy said to me. '*The war started months ago.*'

Three large vehicles - mammoths of engineering supported by eight tyres - drive along the main pathway nearest to the explosion. I think they're heading in the direction of the quad and administration complex.
There are close to two-hundred soldiers in each, all sitting in the back trailers. Some adjust the straps on their bullet-resistant vests, some hastily put their helmets on, others check to make sure their weapons are fully loaded. They were obviously called to action moments after the catastrophic blast and given minutes, maybe even less, to prepare for duty.

"This is why they're so scared," says the boy in a low voice. His wide eyes sparkle and he forces a smile, despite the pain in his lip. "This is why they run around like armed rats! They fear it ... they fear any change or threat to their power ... their control!"

He knows so much ... has he seen this in other parts of the world?

"Don't worry." The boy grabs my wrist with a gentle grasp as he shakes his head. "We aren't under attack. I caused the explosion."

I stare in disbelief. *You did ... what?* There are vocal words, questions as well, yet they can't escape. *You started all this? One boy can cause all this damage ... all this chaos? You ... you are one person, one boy ... and you dared to fight?*

"How?" I manage to ask as I stand up. My legs are suddenly full of strength and energy. A new, powerful, and raw emotion floods through me like a surge of electricity rising up from my feet. "Tell me. Please?"

I want to know everything about M-532 ... every story he could possibly tell me. I want to see the world through his eyes. I want to climb inside his very skin and become him, absorb his spirit, his confidence. I need everything from him I do not own.

I return to the thought which I previously refused to believe as the truth. *He acted scared! I was right! He wanted anyone who might see him to believe his behaviour ... It was all an act ... a fake reaction to the blast!*

I notice a soldier is walking towards us both with his rifle held in a tight grip. I have to try and curb my new feelings.

The boy stands up and keeps talking, although he conceals any lip movements under his hand. "I cut the gas line in the kitchen. As soon as Darius ordered us both to leave, I knew we'd be safely out of the building. I took my chance ..."

"Halt!" barks the soldier as he reaches us. His muscular frame stands directly in front of the sun. It casts his whole body as a shimmering silhouette - a hulking monster of blurred darkness. "This area is not safe. Why are you both here?"

The boy remains silent and keeps his hand over the cut running across his upper lip. The fact he has been injured won't stop him from being struck with the back of a hand, or a baton, if he fails to provide a valid reason.

Answer him, now!

I remember the incident in the kitchen and how the boy's silence had provoked Darius to become violent.

I move forward with a single step, taking the soldier's attention towards myself. He carries two bronze insignia on his left lapel - Corporal rank - and the name *Taber* has been sewn on the front of his dark-green tunic.

"We were on our way to the hospital when the explosion occurred. This boy has been injured and I am due for harv ..."

"Enough ... enough!" Corporal Taber waves his hand so I will stop talking. My voice seems to anger, or annoy, him and he doesn't want to listen any longer.

He presses a finger against an earpiece he is wearing so he can listen to situation updates and any new orders. His broad and straight shoulders relax by an inch or two and the urgent glaze disappears from over his brown eyes.

"Understood. Yes, sir."

We'll be sent back to our cells, won't we? Warden Horrell doesn't usually need an excuse or a reason to order a lock down.

Corporal Taber turns around and signals to a nearby member from his platoon: a tall female with the name Dunstan on her uniform. She runs over to our position to hear the latest order.

"We have a battalion, four-hundred strong, in a perimeter line around the administration complex. We need to supply back up for the fire crews on scene. Preliminary reports suggest it was an isolated incident, even unrelated, but we won't know the exact cause until the fire investigators have studied the scene."

"Understood, Corporal. What of the sightings towards the coast?"

"Activity from the mainland, and out at sea, is being closely monitored. They aren't advancing, well, not yet. We're preparing other platoons to secure all routes."

Advancing? People are out there, trying to reach us? Are they going to attack?

"An announcement for this lot …" Corporal Taber flicks his head with rude indifference backwards in our direction, "… is due any second."

A high-pitched wail from the domain wide klaxons blares a two-tone, continuous, warning. The screens on the dome fade in from black once again to show Warden Horrell's wrinkled face. She peers out over Europa-Four, over her personal empire, as if watching it from the sky. Every person is surrounded by her grip. It reminds us that her eyes are all seeing, her presence complete and unrestricted, her power unchallenged..

"All females, eight-hundred through to nine-five-zero … I repeat, females, eight-hundred through to nine-five-zero.

You will proceed to platform four on the Brunel mainline, immediately. The military personnel on site will instruct you further on arrival."

Why are we going to one of the train stations? Are we to be evacuated out of Europa-Four, away from the danger?

I have no choice but to push the ridiculous thought out of my mind. No compassion is given towards us or placed on our lives. The slaves across the world, we are an expendable commodity, at times a living currency, grown every day to satisfy the global demand.

Warden Horrell's eyes flick downwards as she checks the printed data on a piece of paper. "All males, four-hundred through to five-nine-nine ... males, four-hundred through to five-nine-nine. Proceed to the Equatorial Hub."

I still don't understand! Why are we being sent to different train stations? The Equatorial Hub links to the Atlantic cities ...

I notice something after Warden Horrell has spoken, including both of our identifiers in her list: the boy has lost his impressive resolution, and some of the blue sparkle, the vibrant life force, has drained from his eyes. The unseen hand of those in control has somehow reached inside of him and ripped it out of his body. He displayed such courage and vigour when speaking of the war, yet it has vanished, torn away in an instant.

Why has he changed so much? Does he know something? Does he know what is about to happen to him ... to all of us?

I want nothing more than to drift away, to take myself and my mind to another location. I crave normality, not the opposite of the set routine I have been forced to follow for so many years. I am infected with fear. It crawls under my skin and I know of no cure.

Corporal Taber turns away so he can listen to another transmission. His voice is inaudible as he nods every few seconds.

The boy extends his hand by a few inches. He touches my wrist and the side of my hand with tender fingers. "I'm sorry." He whispers the words as his eyes travel.

I am familiar with such an expression, I have carried it in my own eyes before. He is not focusing on a place, he is trying to find a time instead. He's searching for a specific memory.

"Why?" I ask, finding myself lodged between curiosity and dread, as if two equally powerful magnets are fighting over me, trying to drag me closer. "Why are you sorry?"

Corporal Taber grabs his security baton and pushes it between our bodies. He strikes us both with strong whips and moves us in opposite directions. "You two, get moving!" he shouts.

I should react to the pain but I can't, it's a blocked action. My head is swirling, I feel physically sick, and my hands are still shaking.

Will I see him again?

I have no choice but to walk away, robbed of my chance to speak, to receive an answer, or ask the boy any other questions.

I look back a couple of times as I head along the pathway, hoping to see a signal, perhaps a mouthed word … anything from the boy. It doesn't happen, though, and M-532 disappears amongst the smoke and chaos.

Chapter three

As I approach the Brunel train station, I'm still reeling, in both the physical and emotional sense, from my encounter with M-532.

Hundreds of loud, organised, and well-drilled soldiers are present, as are the lower ranked security staff. I think of the boy again and his comment about rats scurrying about with weapons.

This is an integral sector on Europa-Four, linking it directly with the Britannic Isles. It is named in honour of Isambard Kingdom Brunel, its creator and designer, a celebrated civil engineer from the nineteenth century. Due to my early education, I know he was gifted with an incredible scope and imagination. The train station has managed to keep this title through the subsequent years, mainly due to the reverence placed on Brunel and his significance in world history.

Nearly two-hundred-and-fifty years ago, he designed the train tracks, the fixed platforms anchored to the seabed, even the ships that acted as temporary mooring stations during construction. The first train line to join two countries - running between London, Old England and Dieppe, France -

became operational shortly before Brunel's death.

His vision to unite the world continued as the years, decades, and centuries stacked on top of each other. Just as Brunel's trains powered along tracks, the world completely embraced change and pushed forward with ever increasing feats of architectural and mechanical wonder. Bridges were raised, cities built, and more countries were sewn together with the potent bond of iron and steam, commerce, progression, and profit.

I arrive at the train station and stop walking as I reach the large archway towering over the entrance. Twisted steel rises twenty feet above me on both sides, designed to look like trees and branches sprouting from the ground. It is a welded masterpiece, commissioned and placed solely to greet and impress all who visit here.

I should admire it, or be impressed by the glistening metal as it welcomes the sun's rays, yet my life does not allow for such marvellous fantasy. Everything I see is clouded, corrupted, and impure.

A month old memory resurfaces and I wince with conditioned pain as I look at the knuckles on my hands. *I thought the scars would be much worse. I drifted that day ... I drifted away to the orchard and blocked out the pain ...*

The last time I worked here, one of my tasks involved scrubbing the glorious archway. Many of us had been assigned cleaning duties - it had to be perfect for an upcoming visit from an official mainland delegation. The cleaning supervisor had high, almost unassailable, standards. Nobody could ever reach them. Whether or not she felt extra pressure that morning because of the visit, I don't know. I received ten strikes with a wooden stick across my hands as an immediate and sharp punishment.

I walk again, passing by the thick steel girders and joists, wanting to turn back, even if I don't know exactly why. *What are you so scared of? What do you believe will happen here?*

Platform four is buzzing with activity and an audible soup of different noises greets me: engines, voices, radio transmissions, and static. My sense of hearing filters out most of it and focuses on the muffled cries of the terrified. I am drawn to the suffering of my own kind.

I find myself surrounded by hundreds of other female slaves of various ages. Some are very young ... *too young:* ten or eleven years old and straight out of the basic education camps situated in Octant five.

One of the older women hobbles around, unsure of where to stand, too unsettled by the explosion and its consequences. She has grey hair and light-green eyes, with a thin and short frame. Her back hunches over and her body seems to favour the right leg, pulling it over - in an uncomfortable manner - to one side.

Warden Horrell stands by an armoured vehicle, checking the contents of one of the metal crates stacked inside, of which there are hundreds. She delegates with hand gestures as compliant soldiers hurry about like worker and drone ants, eager to respond and please their queen, moving the crates through the doors of the train carriages.

Horrell is here? Why? What is in those crates?

A soldier pushes me in the back with a sharp jab of his rifle barrel. "Don't just stand there!" he says.

"Sorry, sir." I mumble my apology.

Another jab steers me towards a slow moving line of girls on the left side of the platform. I don't walk fast enough for the soldier and his heavy fist cracks me on the shoulder.

Some of the females hold back tears, some keep turning their heads left and right, trying to work out why they are being herded around like cattle. Many of us have worked on the farms inside Octant eight, and the adjoining slaughterhouses, although I haven't for a couple of years. I can understand why the similarities hatch incredible fear in all their young imaginations: they are being led away to die, pushed to the end of their existence, walked towards a machine that will stun the life from their bodies.

I can't remember anything similar happening to me before. How could I? I have never experienced war. I think of the boy again: M-532, and his elusive, mesmerising words. *Is this how war feels? Are we being sent out to ... to fight? Am I now a soldier?*

"Listen up! All of you!" Warden Horrell stands higher than everyone else on the side of the armoured vehicle.

To me, she appears as a dominant statue, a figurehead of the system.

"You will now be taken along the train tracks. The soldiers will give you instructions once you reach your destination!"

Where? Are we going to the mainland?

Before Warden Horrell walks away, I hear her instruct members of a squad of soldiers to move the vehicles full of crates to each of the other train stations. Her face has never been so concrete, so emotionless. She has a single, albeit unknown, purpose. Her eyes jump left and right as she calculates veiled manoeuvres inside her mind.

I wish I could hear your thoughts ... I wish I could see inside that darkened mind of yours, just for a second ...

I walk through the carriage doors and find a gap next to a young girl with light-brown skin and hazel eyes. We both turn away from the accompanying soldiers and smile at each other, offering the unspoken support that is so common amongst the slaves. An entire, and very secretive, language, created without any words.

I look down to her arm. She is inked with F-802 and twelve dots, one of which looks recent and extremely sore.

Twelve years old and so scared ...

A tear falls down the girl's cheek so she wipes it away, afraid that her emotions will earn a swift punishment.

We're all scared, trust me. I wish I could help you more ... but ... I don't know how ...

As the automatic doors slide shut, a female voice fills

the carriage, broadcasting through the internal speaker system. "Stand in lines with your right wrist held out. You are all to be issued and fitted with an emergency tracking beacon. Once in place, do not attempt to remove it from your wrist."

The boy ... he caused this reaction ... this panic! He changed, though, became scared ... told me he was sorry. Has he worn one of these tracking devices before?

The air changes as we leave the dome. It becomes pure, real, not ventilated and filtered like inside Europa-Four. I don't get to experience the world outside very often - the *true* world outside - because my duties don't warrant it. Perhaps now, with the onset of war, we will all be forced out from under the dome, from our caged and regulated life?

The train journey lasts for about ten minutes, although I estimate this. I have no real sense of time and can only use a counting method in my head, or compare it to past duties. I know it takes me ten minutes to clean the oven in the kitchens - any longer and I will be punished. I feel as if I have had enough time to clean an oven.

I now have a heavy steel cuff locked around my wrist, as do all the other female slaves. It has two lit LEDs on the surface: blue and green. *What are these for? Why would they need to track us?*

The carriage slows to a gentle speed. For an unknown reason, I notice all the soldiers in here with us - ten in total - are listening to an update through their earpieces. I don't understand why this interests me so much. *Or, is it fear? Do I fear what their instructions could be?*

As we come to a stop, the speaker system clicks and whines with feedback. "Everyone out! Follow the soldiers and form lines as designated along the platform!"

The female voice appears with such a sudden clarity, it causes my body to jump and tense up.

Calm down! I tell myself as I step off the train. We haven't travelled the full distance to the Britannic Isles, stopping instead at one of the maintenance areas. The tracks are lower here, bringing everyone closer to the sea, only one-hundred feet above the surface of the water.

Once again, I feel a rifle barrel in my back, plus a tight and overly forceful hand around my upper arm. We are all pushed, directed, and positioned from one side of the platform to the other.

The soldiers are working so ... efficiently. Did Warden Horrell have this planned? Have the soldiers been trained for this?

Soon, we have all created a long line of confused bodies a few feet apart, standing like a line of pawns in a large game of chess. We don't know the players and we will never fully comprehend the rules.

The sun feels warm on my skin even though it is still low in the sky. I let it calm me as I am placed directly by the railing on the left side, listening to the soft sway of the sea beneath me. I catch glimpses of it out of the corner of my eye. It looks inviting. I will add this to my imagination, as of this very moment, and drift here when I need to. I shall now be able to escape and swim, or float in the sea.

One of the soldiers, a corporal, walks ahead of our line and studies the distance with a pair of binoculars. He looks down the train line for half a minute, then signals for another soldier to join him. He adjusts the magnification setting and looks again.

"They're down there, watching us as we watch them ... but ... no offensive activity. Get the rest of the platoon ready to move back."

"Yes, Corporal Vieira!" says the other soldier. She spins around on her thick boots and marches back towards the train carriage.

They? Other people? I peer and squint, trying to focus my eyes. It only makes me realise how tired they feel. My body aches as well because I have been awake for hours already. Before my kitchen duties began at five, I was in the laundry, washing, drying, and ironing clothes.

A dot of light sparkles for a few seconds … then another … another … the sun has found something to reflect off.

'They're down there, watching us as we watch them.' *Corporal Vieira just said those words.*

I stare forwards again, ignoring the tired strain in my eyes. *Is that what I can see?*

Shapes emerge, blurry and distant yet dark enough for me to recognise. It is a line of vehicles and smaller shapes moving about … people. *Who are they? Why have they brought trucks along the train lines?*

Corporal Vieira turns around to face us all. "Stay here until further notice. Do not adjust your positions. Remain in your lines!"

I watch as the soldiers all walk away and board the train carriages again. More sparkles of light flash in the distance. The whirr from the electricity on the overhead line above the train hums and the carriages move away.

Within minutes, we are all alone. Not one of us speaks a word, yet tears fall, hands shake, and hearts thump with rapid beats. None of us can imagine a positive scenario because our lives are, ultimately, negative. We are born, raised and controlled … and we are given no choice or means to change such a crushing and lonely fact.

"I've seen this before! I've seen this before!" screams a voice. It is the old woman with grey hair and light-green eyes. I remember her because of the erratic behaviour she displayed earlier on the platform. "We're … we're …"

What is she doing? Corporal Vieira told us not to move! Stay here! Stay in line!

I fear this woman will fall at any second. Somewhere behind us, hidden in a strategic location, there will be a sniper.

"We're all going to die!" shrieks the old woman. She taps at her head once again and pulls at the cuff on her wrist. "Get this off! Get this off me!"

Her weak and deformed legs hobble forward fifty-feet, heading for the side barrier. She squeezes herself through the gap in the metal railings - with considerable effort - then hits her tracking device down hard on top of it.

What do I do? Should I stop her? I stand perfectly still, unable to pick a clear course of action. I'm arguing with myself and the indecision it creates tenses up all my muscles.

The old woman balances on the outer ledge of the platform. She has only a few inches of steel under her feet to perch on. *Hold the railing! Why won't you hold on?*

One of her hands pulls and scratches at the tracking beacon on her wrist, the other keeps tapping on her temple in a repetitive pattern. "Boom-boom! You're dead! Boom-boom!" she says and her voice is nothing more than a croaky wheeze.

A gust of air blows across the platform, as if the weather itself wants to keep the old woman safe. It wants to push her frail body back over the metal railing.

The sparkles of light multiply. More pairs of binoculars are watching. The blurred vehicles start to move closer soon after.

NO!

The old woman disappears off of the steel girder and falls to the sea. I still don't move. My legs feel heavy and produce pulses of fear, surging in powerful jolts. Even if I want to leave my position on the platform, I don't think I could manage it. It's physically impossible.

Wait! She's ... alive! I can hear the old woman splashing and yelling in the sea below, thrashing at the water with agitated swipes of her arms and hands.

I am about to smile. I want the old woman to be safe, to be alive. *Will the soldiers come back to rescue her?*

Then, a plume of water shoots up out of the sea, spraying tiny droplets and a fine mist through the air ... water which now has a red and pink tint running through it. I can't hear the old woman.

Was that ... was that blood? What happened? Did the people further down the tracks ... shoot her? No, wait ... there must have been an explosion to cause the water to shoot up in the air ... an explosion ... an explosive device ... a mine in the water?

A sickening thought enters my head as I stare. I slam a mental door and lock it shut, using fear - infinite and all consuming fear - as the key and padlock. My eyes betray me, though, and steal a forbidden glance at the cuff on my wrist.

I'm distracted because the trucks stop and I can clearly see people. They are rushing about across the platform. Some are looking over the railings, some kneeling down, holding ... rifles.

No! Please, no! My heart jumps as I imagine a bullet ripping through my body at any second.

Before I can piece all the parts of the jigsaw together in my mind, a thud rocks the metal panels under my feet. It happens twice more before an explosion rips through the train tracks, one-hundred-and-fifty metres away. *Are we under attack? Is this it? Is this ... the war?*

I can't decide if Corporal Vieira will return. *He should join the fight, shouldn't he? Or, will he leave us here instead? Was that the plan all along?*

I remember all the soldiers in the train carriage, listening to their earpieces as we arrived here. Were their orders similar to my own thoughts?

The breeze returns to blow the smoke from the explosion away. The train tracks are buckled, snapped, and there is a visible gap across the platform, now separating us from the mainland. I see something ... a clear shape climbing over the railings ... it is a young woman.

Your hair ... it's ... long? You aren't wearing clothes like me ... like all the slaves. How can you be so different?

The young woman stands in a defiant stance as the breeze carries the last wisps of smoke away from the platform. Her hair looks to be a glowing burgundy, hanging low over her shoulders. I think she is wearing brown boots, beige trousers covered in pockets, and a black coat that looks to be made of leather. The sun bounces off of the lines and creases on it, forcing every pair of eyes to stare, to see her, to remember her. I am not the only one standing here in shock. I am not the only one to be put under a spell by the appearance of this woman.

Who are you?

I feel the same emotions which filled me earlier this morning. They rush back with force and a clear intent: to change me. To push my mind to break through the wall. I want to become this young woman, to know her, to experience her entire life. I need to hear her words, see her eyes, and let her see mine. I wish for every thought in her mind to float through the air and join with my own. I want her to teach me all that she knows.

I make a conscious effort to stay still. My legs twitch, eager to sprint forward. I will leap across the destroyed platform if it means I get to be near her.

Two of the trucks have made their way up the train tracks after the explosion, yet still keep their distance a couple of hundred feet behind the young woman. She turns, realising it is time for her to leave. Her mission is over.

What are you doing now?

The young woman decides there is something else to show us all before she joins the trucks. She pulls her arm out of her coat sleeve and holds it up in the air.

I can't see the movements in perfect detail, due to the distance, but it appears as if she is drawing an imaginary line on her skin, up and down … up and down. I look down at my own arm. I study the letter, numbers, and dots. I gaze back at the young woman …

I feel something light and gentle on my cheek … it's a tear. It rolls slowly down my face.

She's … she's crossing out her ink … she doesn't need an identifier … she won't be branded …

Another tear falls, followed by a few more. I have no power to stop them. I am too weak and feel so tired, so drained of all my energy.

It's true … She is … free …

Chapter four

I want to sink to my knees in a flood of tears. My physical body is weak and being controlled by another part of me, a powerful and unnamed master. It could be my subconscious, or something much deeper and enigmatic … my life force, or my soul.

Despite my own emotional resistance, I manage to wipe my eyes dry and force more tears to stop falling.

The soldiers are coming back!

I can hear the hum of electricity growing louder behind me on the train line. I should turn around but my glazed eyes are only interested in the young woman and the ink on my forearm.

I can't imagine how the military will react when they arrive on the scene. This is an unprecedented situation and there is a tiny spark inside of me that is terrified. It sits next to another which yearns to grow and ignite, waiting and begging to spread like an uncontrollable and raging fire.

If others feel this way, can I?

At its most basic level, my life has taught me to be controlled, to obey. All the punishments and mental abuse cannot remove the feelings of want and need, though. I know

I want and need to be like these other people, M-532, and the young woman, more than anything else. Their actions make me believe I can do something I've never thought about before: *fight back.*

As the train carriages reach us, the young woman walks off towards the trucks at a calm pace. She knows the soldiers can see her, yet it doesn't seem to matter. She dares to flaunt her recent success in their faces. The whole scene is a piece of theatre, orchestrated as a declaration and a powerful statement. *The world is changing. We're changing your world ... and you can't stop us!*

Corporal Vieira's authority erupts as soon as his heavy boots thump down on the platform. He shouts frantic orders and his commanding presence drags the situation under control, forcing all the thoughts from my mind - all the rebellion and defiance inside. I won't forget them, it will be impossible now.

The soldiers move around in a drilled formation, across and down the platform, weaving an armed web. A small squad breaks off and begins to march me and all the other females back to the carriages, while others take sheltered vantage points near to the explosion further down the tracks.

It's ... true! We are at war ... I am walking through a war zone!

The hectic scenes cloud my overstimulated senses, there are too many voices and people moving about. I feel disoriented as I stare out of the window, trying to absorb as much detail and information as I can. It is like a dream: blurry and vague with images scattering themselves all around me. I can't focus on one situation long enough for it to register before another wrenches my attention away.

Armed rats, I think as I wonder if I'll ever see the boy again. I need him to tell me more, to answer all of my questions.

The train starts to move away from the chaos,

transporting us all back towards Europa-Four. It is full of silence and fear, full of hidden and controlled emotions. Since the train tracks were blown apart, it is the first time I've acted unselfishly and thought of the others with me.

Do they feel as I do? Confused and exhilarated at the same time?

I can't see F-802, the girl I stood with on the journey here. Her naïve expression from the journey here returns to my mind and grounds me, as if she has somehow pulled me away from the confusion. *Please, don't be too scared by what has happened. Be strong, that's all you can be ...*

One of the nearby soldiers receives an order through his earpiece. "Understood, sir," he says after a few seconds.

I am near the back of the carriage. The soldier walks to the woman next to me and removes her tracking beacon first, then mine. He places them back in the crate on the floor before walking away to remove the cuffs off of the other females. His face and eyes show a cocktail of emotions I can't read: wide pupils, clammy skin, and subtle movements in his jaw as he grinds his teeth together.

The thought I locked away earlier attacks the mental door with a couple of forceful kicks. It needs to be heard again and I am willing to listen. My recent memory jolts so I see the old woman's eyes as she scratched at her wrist. Those light-green eyes knew something ... they feared something.

Could they really be explosives? If the others ... those from the mainland ... if they came too close, would Corporal Vieira have used them ... used us ... like that?

••

As I arrive back at the Brunel train station, I see a female soldier. Through the carriage window, I still notice her blue eyes scanning left and right, rigid shoulders, and alert body stance. She is standing on the platform with a tight grip on her automatic rifle ... and fear across her face.

As the carriage door slides open, I can feel my heart beating faster. I'm unsure, yet I think it is caused by excitement, an emotion my body is usually unfamiliar with. I want to gloat and vent these new experiences for all to hear and see.

I've never seen conflict before. All the military and security will be frightened by the thought of war as well. They are used to controlling the slaves around the world, spreading fear, and physical pain, to those who can't defend themselves. Now, their enemies retaliate. I have no sympathy for any of them. Let them live as I do, every single day! Let them answer for their choices and actions!

"Warden Horrell has ordered a lock-down until further notice!" the soldier shouts. "Disembark and return to your cells! Follow the secure path at all times!"

I knew this would happen ... Will we be told the truth about the war? It can't be hidden any longer, can it? We've seen too much now ...

Our route back to the cell block building is lined with security officers. They are positioned twenty to thirty feet apart, marking the path, all armed with handguns and batons. I'm surprised to see military vehicles have been parked every few hundred feet as well, full of ammunition crates.

Europa-Four looks and feels so different now despite the fact I haven't been away for very long. It is still a machine, it is still grinding and moving, yet it has begun to evolve. It has become a living entity, an animal protecting itself from dangerous predators.

I keep my gaze low, looking at the pathway under my feet with deliberate intent. I don't know how those in power might react to the war reaching their city, or how it will change them. Instinct tells me I should disappear if I wish to stay safe, blend in and not invite or encourage attention towards myself - for any possible reason.

After an hour, possibly more, of marching at a difficult speed - one regulated by the security guards - I reach the cell block areas in Octant five. My leg muscles feel as if they are ready to explode or cramp up, burning and stinging with every step.

My block has a large *D* stencilled on the side of it in black paint. In total, close to one-hundred thousand slaves are housed here, crammed inside four tall buildings. They are spread out in a crossed design and shape, with the males and females separated. In reality, these are just oversized metal boxes in which Warden Horrell can lock us away. The drab steel panels on the outside reflect the interior mood so well, using a strange power within them to depress those who pass through the thick doors. The sight of this place always pulls and squeezes at my heart with a crushing grip.

I have experienced lock-downs before several times in my life and they remind me - not that I ever need reminding - of the true value of a slave. Just under a year ago, a group of dignitaries from the Equatorial regions toured Europa-Four. Warden Horrell locked a huge number of us away for two whole days. The visitors didn't care for slaves at all and didn't even want to witness our existence. It was as if we would spoil the visit by letting their privileged eyes fall on us. Unworthy beings such as us shouldn't ever be seen. Some slaves still had to work behind the scenes: cooking, cleaning, and running essential tasks, yet they were kept out of view.

Once the dignitaries had returned to their own part of the world, our duties increased so we could reclaim the lost hours of work. Many were beaten during that time.

I climb the final few steps on the steel stairs and make my way along the metal grid walkway of level four. My cell, 412, is open, awaiting my arrival.

"Inside. Food and water has been left for you," says a tall guard. He walks to the next cell and repeats the statement to another female.

Food!? I shout in my mind.

It is nothing more than a grey and tasteless sludge,

which meets an archaic dietary allowance. It contains all the minerals and vitamins required to keep a person from starving to death, although the official health statement and ingredients sound much more humane.

How long will I be here for this time? Are we to be shut away for the entire war?

There are no windows in the cell blocks. My sense of time is non-existent after the cascading events of this morning. I remember the sun being high in the sky before I walked in the building.

••

Despite being a slave, I do not spend a lot of time in my cell. I work, we all do, for lengthy periods, then sleep for a few hours before the cycle starts again. I am usually awake and carrying out my duties for eighteen hours a day, although more is not uncommon. This is another reason why lock-downs cause such resentment and fear: the last fragment of our freedom is taken away. The ability to walk about on Europa-Four is revoked and all that takes its place is a cold and square room.

I have seen people lose their minds while inside these walls. I've listened to the screams of those begging to be released, the sickening sounds as punches of soft and weak fists and feet hit the steel walls. After lock-downs, I often notice the new cuts and bruises on others when we are finally released. Some can't withstand the isolation.

I use routines and methods - ones created to keep me sane and distracted. Sometimes I exercise, or I count the bolts in the walls and panels beneath my feet. As long as I don't let myself suffocate with thoughts of imprisonment, I can survive long periods of cell time. I have drifted away inside this prison on numerous occasions ... floating through the bars and away to freedom.

I eat, drink, and let the confinement begin, then, I set

my routine and repeat it to myself at least fifty times - I don't need to but it's about ten minutes wasted. One deliberate omission is sleep, although I probably should take this opportunity to rest. I know I won't be able to, not right now. I have so many questions running through my mind, I need to be awake to try and answer them.

I start to walk from one side of my seven-square-foot foot cell to the other.

You need to do this one-hundred times, that is your first task.

This will give me the opportunity to think about the boy, M-532, and the initial explosion. I am also going to count the number of steps the security guards take on their patrols around the level, that will be my second task.

The boy caused the explosion ... and he knows of the war. He told me that he's worked in other parts of the world ... did those countries fall? Is that how and why he ended up here?

"Nine-zero-zero to nine-four-nine!" shouts a voice. A loud klaxon follows as security personnel bang on cell bars with their batons. Even though I chose not to, some of the females in here must have taken their chance to sleep.

I've only been back for thirty minutes, at the most! Where are they taking me now?

"You are all to be escorted to the hospital for fertilisation harvesting. We leave immediately!"

A security guard appears in front of me and waits for the cell door to slide open. He looks stern and emotionless, they always do, but I can see the fear in his eyes. It is spreading through all of them like a virus, infecting host after host.

Chapter five

The hospital complex is situated close by on the outer edge of Octant five, a short distance from the cell blocks. A large unit, one which barely qualifies as sterile, is the one and only facility here for all the slaves. All the rest are used by military, staff, and residents ... *the ones who matter*.

Those living in the administration complex never come here, they use a private hospital inside their secluded quarter of Europa-Four instead. I've seen it from the outside on a number of occasions, yet have never been permitted to enter. It is a luxurious brick building, secluded by the edge of the dome and surrounded by landscaped gardens.

The remaining buildings are designated for research and development ... and ... experiments. Many of the nightmares that visit me, when I do sleep, are created here. My life is one of suffering, one of oppression and pain, but for the slaves chosen to assist in the *advancement of science* ... I can't imagine their lives, and don't ever want to. I pity them and wish for painless and quick deaths, it is the only humane thought I can have. My work in the laboratories brings a torturous cloud with it. I pack prescription medicines or vaccines, and push crates around on a trolley, all while listening to the screams from *volunteers*.

I feel sick ...

I know this upcoming medical procedure all too well and hold a fear towards it ... no, not a fear ... it's more of a foreboding anxiety, a loathing. I dread the thought of it - and everything it represents - even though I have been subject to it since reaching puberty. A barrage of blood tests and physical examinations proved I was fertile enough to be used for harvesting. I, albeit unwillingly, will assist in the creation of new slaves. In a little under a year's time, my ... my offspring ... *my children* ... they could be suspended inside the amniotic tanks which line the two largest buildings here in the complex. They are referred to by staff as 'the nest'. Tens of thousands of chambers are stacked together in rows and columns, filled with new, oppressed life.

Of course, fertilization and slave breeding are complex. The harvested eggs could in fact sit for years before being matched in the database and retrieved for use. A computer system must calculate a successful outcome before the process is initiated. Another remarkable breakthrough in mankind's history, one which has helped so many in the past, now degraded and darkened to serve those in power.

This is the main reason I feel sick and why I am so anxious. *And this is why the young woman created that spark inside me! They shouldn't be allowed to use me in this way!*

I walk through the automatic doors with the other females, recognising my own expression on their horrified faces.

"Next!" orders a male member of staff. He has blond hair and a low voice. I don't see his eyes because he doesn't even bother to lift his head and look at me.

I hold out my arm underneath the scanner and wait for a beep of confirmation. The man taps at his computer keyboard before pointing me to the left hallway.

Calm down ... you've done this before ... you shouldn't feel so sick ... so afraid ... I think as I walk to the main ward.

There are thousands of beds here, running in eight neat lines, with a white curtain around each of them. I tune out as best as I can to dampen the noise and dull the moment.

"Remove your clothes. Up on the table," says the nurse on duty as I reach an empty bed with the number 743 above it. She is a middle aged woman with straight black hair, brown eyes, and welcoming features. I recognise her from previous visits and my nausea subsides, yet only slightly.

At least you are gentle ... you care, even though you shouldn't.

I take off my shirt, trousers, and shoes, then notice the new bruise on my shoulder.

The punch on the platform this morning ... I wonder if Corporal Taber's baton did the same to my back?

"Come on, hurry up!" says the nurse. "Take this while I prepare the machines. You're here for a lot longer today. We need extra stock." She points to a tablet on the tray at the end of the bed.

I know these are manufactured in the laboratories. A single dose will ensure my body ... *obeys the rules*. The bodies of all the females are treated in exactly the same way: the medication forces them to ovulate.

"I understand," I say as my stomach flips over a couple of times.

I climb on the bed, swallow my pink tablet with a small sip of provided water, then pull the thin white sheet up over my chest. It feels cold in the hospital today, more than usual, so I dream for a moment about the orchard and sunlight cutting through the leaves on the trees. At least there are windows here, unlike my cell block. Light is allowed to enter and roam about inside this building, filling spaces with warmth.

I sit up and look around at all the faces, trying to read their thoughts from a single expression. This is a time when every detail stays with me. Even when I escape and drift away, I remember everything from my visits here. Every beep of the machines, every surgical tool touching my skin, and the nausea that has plagued me since this began nearly six years ago.

"Heating is rationed. Warden Horrell has initiated some emergency measures after ....," says the nurse as she returns with a portable ultrasound unit and an array of long needles and tubes. She places them on the tray at the end of the bed and then breaks her smile. "Oh, what am I explaining it to you for? If you're cold, you're cold. Tough!"

I didn't say anything! I look away.

The nurse, herself in shock due to the events of this morning, must have momentarily forgotten her place in the hierarchy. She wants to talk to someone, it is only natural, she has fears to share just like everyone else.

The cubicles usually only hold one female at a time, so I am surprised when another arrives on a bed a few seconds later. She is wheeled in by a red-faced porter, mid-fifties, with wispy blond hair. He looks exhausted and his eyes are bloodshot with distinctive patches under them on the skin.

"I've got another seven waiting at reception. Where do you want them?" he asks.

The nurse rolls her eyes. "Seven? What is happening in here today?" she says and leaves with the flustered porter, closing the curtain behind her.

Has Warden Horrell ordered the staff to work harder? Has she changed their lives in the last few hours?

A strange side-effect from the war forms in my mind. *I wonder if the staff and residents can leave Europa-Four? Are they allowed to transfer to another country or city, or are they imprisoned now, like me? It would explain why the nurse seems so agitated.*

"Hel ... hello ..." says a timid and low voice.

I roll my head to the side and smile with a gentle compassion. I am not alone in my fear and disdain for the upcoming medical procedure.

The girl has dark-brown hair and soft blue eyes. They sparkle with an amazing and magical contrast against her brown skin. The fact that her hair is only a couple of inches long doesn't seem to matter as it suits the round shape of her face. She has fourteen dots and F-1211 inked on her forearm. I know I've seen her walking out of cell block D in the past.

"After a while, you'll get used to it. There's no need to be scared ... you've ... you've had this done before, yes?" I ask. I want to reach across and hold her tiny hand but am worried the nurse will disapprove.

F-1211 nods with the same loathing which is causing my nausea. "I don't care about this," she says. "I'm just ... frightened ... after what happened this morning."

"I think we all are." I pause for a second and listen to the approaching footsteps. They change direction and head away to the right.

"Do you ... know what happened?" the girl whispers.

"I saw the explosion! I was in the kitchen just before it was destroyed!" I say and it is difficult to keep my voice low. My words are desperate to be heard.

The girl's mouth opens as she takes a sharp breath in.

"Immediately afterwards, they sent me to the Brunel train line with others. Were you taken anywhere?" I say and realise I'm speaking quickly.

The opportunity to talk with someone else about this morning fills me with an unusual and unexpected thrill. I think back to the security guard outside my cell with fear in his eyes ... he had been infected by it. I feel as if I am helping the virus - the fear - I'm spreading it through Europa-Four by simply talking to this girl.

She sits up, leans towards me, and the edges of her lips turn down. "Did you all have to wear the metal cuffs?" she asks.

I am slightly stunned by the question and pause as I try to work out why she has asked me. "You mean the tracking beacon?"

The girl's eyes widen and she looks towards the white curtain around our beds, checking again for any nearby staff. "On your wrist, yes?"

I nod. "Yes, we all did. There were one-hundred-and-fifty of us to begin with ... but ... we lost one ... she jumped off the platform ..."

"Jumped off?" the girl asks. She speaks too loudly and snaps her head towards the curtain.

I'm not sure I want to talk about this ... I'm not sure I can.

I know the girl wants information and answers, though, just as much as I do. "She became ... I don't know how to explain it. She was mumbling to herself, hitting her own head. She kept trying to pull the cuff off of her wrist ... I definitely remember that," I say and realise the events of this morning have already begun to blur together.

"Anything else?" The girl moves herself in bed once again. Her body language cries that she is eager, as if it is feeding off every single word I say.

I can hear the nurse close by but her voice moves away instead of growing closer. "Erm ... it's a bit vague ... erm ... she said that she had seen it before. Why are you so interested?" I turn the questions back to the girl. If anything it should slow her mind down and stop it racing.

Her eyes stare at the curtain as if a platoon of soldiers might charge in and shoot her on the spot. "They weren't tracking beacons," she says. "They contained explosives!"

The mental door I tried to lock earlier explodes as a million splinters attack my mind. My fears were correct, confirmed by every second I spend with F-1211. "What?" I ask, shocked and reluctant to hear the explanation.

The girl swings her legs around to sit on the edge of her bed. She covers her naked body with the white sheet but I can see bruises and scars all over her legs and arms. "I was sent to a different train line ... on the opposite side of the city. The military ordered ten of our group to walk down the track and wait there for further orders. Once they were a safe distance away, he pressed a button on a mobile communicator and they … they all …"

A pause follows as the girl swallows and closes her eyes. "… disappeared inside the smoke and flames … and the train tracks were damaged at the same time."

NO! "But … that … that's impossible!" I say, even though I believe it without hesitation.

Without realising it, I too have adjusted my body. I am on my knees, leaning towards the girl, drawing everything from her.

I hear a noise behind me … another bed … another female. *Can she hear us? Will she tell others too?* I can almost feel the fear virus crawling across the beds around me.

"Why? Why is it impossible?" the girl asks. It is the first time I see the forced maturity show through and darken her brilliant eyes. She may only be fourteen years old, yet it is obvious the life of a subordinate has already shown her the true and darkest elements of the world … our world … where the slaves crawl through the shadows.

I know I can't answer her. I have no words to justify my claim. It *is* possible. It is exactly how I and the other slaves would be used in a war. We are expendable and now, as this beautiful girl and I have seen, we are walking, living, weapons.

I think … I think I'm going to be sick …

"What are you two talking about? Be quiet! I'm starting in a couple of minutes," the nurse says as she returns with another machine and medical instruments.

She pushes me back down on the bed and my stomach begins to churn over. My thighs and legs tense, expecting the ice cold metallic instruments to touch them at any moment.

Then, the nurse grabs the girl's legs and pulls them around towards the mattress. "No more talking!"

I turn my head to look at F-1211. She is already staring at me, holding me in a trance with those magnificent eyes. We are simply trying to find answers from each other, more details and clues as to what we might face in the days ahead.

The nurse turns on a couple of machines and I recognise the rhythm of their shrill beeps. I ignore them and recall everything since this morning in the kitchen, every detail I can find. I set out every single one of them in my mind: the boy, the old woman on the tracks, how the soldiers and security guards have acted, the girl in the bed next to me … even the nurse's slight change in attitude. People know … slaves know … and the boy spoke an undeniable truth while we stood together on the pathway. '*It will change … one day.*'

You were right … it will … it already has …

I take a deep breath and suppress a hidden smile.

Chapter six

I walk to the dirty and sweat stained mattress - on the floor by the back wall of my cell - and fall down, letting my eyes close and every muscle in my body relax.

When I left the hospital building, I looked at the digital read-out on the wall and couldn't quite believe it: 14:58. *I was in there for hours ...*

I decide not to create a new routine straight away because I still feel sick. My stomach and groin also hurt after the fertilisation harvesting. The usually gentle nurse had forceful hands today instead. She was either rushed, in a bad mood, or a mixture of both.

All I want to do is sleep. *Drift away ... rest now, while you have a chance.*

My mind wants to travel to the orchard and I don't resist the pull. I imagine my body lifting off of the ground by just a few inches and floating forward.

I pass through the cell bars and the steel wall panels ... I am free. I drift through Europa-Four and nobody sees me. I am an ethereal soul, staring at the world, watching it play out around me.

"Up, girl! You have a visitor," orders a security guard outside my cell. "Come on, move!"

My imagination fails and rips me back to the real world with unashamed force. The mattress under my skin feels hot, yet still welcoming, and I have to push myself to sit up. My stomach muscles, already sore from the hospital, pull and twist.

A visitor? Why would anyone want to visit ... oh no ... it's her ...

Warden Horrell appears in front of me and peers through the bars with her searching black eyes. She is silent, deadly, and threatening. For half a minute she stands, without moving or speaking, deliberately building my anxiety and fear. She has a large handgun holstered around her waist with a long and wide barrel, and a machete sheathed on one of her thighs. Her fingers twitch next to both, as if she wants me to give her a reason to use them. Her plaited hair - her scorpion tail - coils down her neck. I imagine it will whip forward and strike me dead at any second.

Warden Horrell takes a deep breath in through her pointed nose, flaring her nostrils out widely. It causes more deep lines to appear on her skin. Her shoulders suddenly widen and I can see her fists clenching. "Open this cell."

Why are you here? Why are you angry with me?

I stand up, as I have been educated to do, unaware of what might happen next. I'm fearing the worst because Warden Horrell, or any of those with power, do not visit slaves for many reasons other than to punish.

"Show me your identifier," says Warden Horrell. She undoes the top button of her grey blazer and wipes her brow. The cell blocks can grow dangerously hot, especially in the summer months.

I hold out my left arm so that Warden Horrell can see the inked numbers.

She grabs it in a tight grip and yanks it towards her, causing me to stumble forward by a few steps. "I want to ask you some very important questions about the explosion this morning."

Oh no! Stay calm! I mustn't let her sense that I'm scared ... "Yes, ma'am."

"Answer all my questions truthfully. Do you understand?"

"Yes, ma'am."

Warden Horrell runs her fingers down my arm and wrist after she speaks. Her thumb and forefinger stop on my hand, an inch below the knuckles. Then, with a spark of contempt in her black eyes, she starts to push.

What ... what are you doing? I feel a crushing and sharp pain in my hand.

"DO-YOU-UNDERSTAND?" Warden Horrell repeats her question with a vindictive squeeze and the faintest of smiles twitching at her lips.

I nod. *You're ... you're enjoying this?* My heart races and my lungs beg for more air. I grit my teeth and breathe in with short and sharp gasps.

Warden Horrell pushes one last time, prolonging the torment, before turning around and pacing back towards the bars.

Don't cry. Don't cry! Fight back ... like you want to! Show her that she won't win! I ignore my thoughts and let a tear fall. I have to show pain.

"The explosion. You were on duty in the kitchen before it happened, yes?" asks Warden Horrell.

I put my hands behind my back and stand up straight, hoping my obedient nature and correct posture will conceal the fact I am massaging my hand. Even though Warden Horrell has stopped digging her nails in, it still stings and feels as if the bones are being crushed together. "Yes, ma'am."

"Why did you leave early?"

"The kitchen manager ordered it, ma'am. I had to escort a boy to the hospital after he suffered an injury. Mr Marnett told me to report for harvesting earlier than scheduled," I say with a clear and concise tone.

"I see. I have no way of verifying this, of course, seeing as Mr Marnett was killed in the blast."

Warden Horrell reaches the cell bars and spins around on the heel of her boots. "Aren't you ... *lucky*. You would have been killed if you had stayed there to complete your shift."

A silent stand off follows. Warden Horrell purses her thin lips and taps on her chin while pacing across the small cell.

Does she ... she know? Has she discovered the truth about the boy? If she knows it was an act of sabotage, then she'll believe I was involved!

"Tell me about the injury you mentioned. What happened to the boy?"

"Mr Marnett struck him, ma'am, for insubordination. His lip split."

As I answer, I see Warden Horrell's hand rest on the top of her gun and my heart explodes inside my chest.

"Did he deserve it?"

What? Of course he didn't! I shout the thoughts, disgusted by the question. I know I have to answer ... I have to lie ... and it has to be convincing. "The executions were being transmitted, ma'am. I did not see the whole incident."

Warden Horrell doesn't shout or show any anger. *Does she believe me?*

"Do you know what the explosion actually was?"

"Ma'am?" I have no idea where Horrell is trying to lead me. I don't want to answer incorrectly and receive a slap across the face, or worse.

Warden Horrell steps forward with two thumping strides until inches away from my face. I can smell recently eaten food and alcohol on her breath.

"Indiscipline!" She shouts the word. She has a skill, a natural gift, for losing her temper in the blink of an eye.

I stand my ground yet show a submissive nature at the same time. It's crucial to my survival. I close my eyes and lower my head in respect.

She must know! But ... has she already seen the boy? Has she punished him? I think, forcing myself to accept the fact he is probably already dead.

"Stand up straight!" Warden Horrell pushes me in the shoulder.

"Yes, ma'am. Sorry, ma'am," I say and correct myself.

"I will not accept indiscipline. I will not have those with rebellious thoughts in their minds ruining this great city of mine, this great world!"

I stay silent. As every millisecond ticks away, I have to decide on my actions. If I react or behave incorrectly, I'm afraid Warden Horrell will grab her machete or gun.

"Guard! Get in here!"

A young female, mid-twenties, appears by the cell bars. She has brown eyes and straight black hair in a ponytail.

I see the name Adams on the front of her uniform and it pulls at my memory.

I recognise you. I carried your belongings off of the train two months ago when you arrived here.

"Yes, ma'am." Adams salutes Warden Horrell after walking in.

"Get this one to the Brunel line. She can assist in the reconstruction. We need those tracks operational before sunrise tomorrow." Just as they had on the platform this morning, Warden Horrell's eyes dance from side to side as she plans out the next one-hundred moves.

You do? Why?

"Understood, ma'am," says Adams.

Warden Horrell takes another extended gaze at me as she steps forward to leave the cell. "Give her a couple of strikes with your baton. These ... *people* ... they need reminding, especially now, about order and rules."

NO! I haven't done anything wrong! Don't hit me! PLEASE!

I prepare myself for the imminent pain by drifting away again to the orchard. It is how I detach myself from the physical reality and misery of punishments and beatings.

I float ... I float out of the cell block to the warm orchard. I'm going to dance and run around the tree trunks, touch the leaves ... taste the fruit. Nobody can harm me here ... nobody can touch me here ... I am free, without restraint, without fear ...

A whispered voice carries through the orchard daydream. It speaks in a soft voice, caring and understanding. "Look at me. You need to look at me, right now. Stay quiet, but look at me."

Why are you here? How can you be with me, in my daydream? Adams appears in my mind, standing by a tree trunk.

I open my eyes. Adams is inches away from me with a finger pressed on her lips.

"Do you have any recent bruises?" she whispers.

I nod, look at my shoulder, then point over it at my back.

Adams looks towards the cell bars. "I've known Warden Horrell to check before. Make sure you scream a couple of times. Scream ... or else she will be back."

What? You're ... you're helping me?

Adams whips her baton out with a strong flick of her wrist and walks towards the mattress. "When I hit it, you scream."

"Who are you, ma'am?" I ask in the meekest of whispers.

Adams stares at me for a couple of seconds with a reassuring smile and a familiar glint in her brown eyes. "You don't call me that," she says. "I'm *not* one of them, that's all you need to know."

Chapter seven

I strongly believe fear exists inside of me, as if it is a dominant entity of my own creation. It lives, breathes, evolves, and pumps through my veins, sickening my body, much like an incurable disease would.

Adams' words, her one line of soft and unexpected words, have purged this fear from my body.

They are here ... with me ... with us. They have infiltrated Warden Horrell's lair, her sacred city, her personal domain.

My heart thumps and screams inside my chest as I stare back at Adams' genuine eyes. I take a few moments to study her face, trying to discover her story, trying to discover how our paths have crossed at this specific moment in time.

I suddenly yearn to drift away and see if I can now break through *that* wall, cross *that* line ... taste true freedom for the first time in my life. The elusive dream I have searched for, and been denied for so long ... is it now a possibility?

For the third time in a single day, I am hypnotised by another person. My new feelings, those usually dormant and untouched, pile on top of each other, urging me to learn more ... to be like these people. They are so different to me in countless ways: courageous, spirited, and enigmatic, plus more I haven't even thought of yet.

Is this who I really am? Have I been unable to change myself and evolve ... until now?

Adams looks at the bruise on my hand and cringes. She rubs a gentle thumb across it. "Follow me. Act as you should. I'll take you to the Brunel line as instructed," she says in a hushed, almost inaudible tone. "There's not enough time, and too much information, but I'll try and explain as much as possible on the way."

I nod with a growing hunger for knowledge - my mind opens, awaiting as much as it can hold.

Adams' hand grips around my upper arm and she walks me out of the cell.

Have I ever known kindness like this before? Has any other person treated me this way ... one who isn't a slave?

We walk in silence along level 4 and down the stairs. Adams doesn't look at me once, or speak a single word.

As we leave through the main steel doors, a horn bellows away to our right, from inside the other female prison, block C, and the male block, A. I turn to see thousands of slaves have been herded outside. Others are being marched out of the buildings by soldiers and guards to join them - at gunpoint or with whips from batons.
It seems that no warning was given either - many are barefoot and some are rushing to put their tops on. The heat inside the cell blocks can be unbearable, as it is today, and this often forces us to remove our clothes. We use them to wipe away the sweat, or as makeshift fans to aerate our stifling cells.

Why does this sight scare me so much?

I cannot stop myself from staring. I picture the executions I am so familiar with - multiplied to a heinous level.

It doesn't make any sense. Why would they kill so many?

There are at least ten large transport trucks in view,

either driving towards or away from the slaves. *Where could they be taking them ... and why?*

I look at Adams, hoping for answers. I want her to reassure me but she doesn't even turn her head.

I can see a man I do not immediately recognise from the administration complex. He is close to the first line of females brought out of block C. He caught my attention because his clothes are similar in style to Warden Horrell's.

Who are you? Are you in control of another sector?

He looks to be in his fifties, is slightly overweight, and has long sideburns with more grey in them than black. His eyes, although not close to me, fill me with dread and caution.

This frightening and unfamiliar man is walking up and down the lines, inspecting the slaves. He stops every few seconds to look random males and females up and down.

I don't like this man. He scares me ...

His eyes scan and study the slaves as if they are pieces of meat, as if they are products at a market that he might purchase. If the goods are not of a certain quality, not manufactured with expert craftsmanship, they are to be tossed aside.

Oh ... no ...

I urge a new thought to disappear because I do not want it there, crawling through my mind, creeping around like a burrowing insect. The war has created so much contradiction inside me that it is difficult to organize my thoughts.

I stand next to Adams, my beacon of hope and kindness, as I watch Warden Horrell and the unknown man demonstrate, and personify, greed and poisonous behaviour.

We're being ... traded? We're being offered up as payment ... as collateral! Who is this man? Why does Warden Horrell need to pay him? What can he offer her in return?

Adams looks around to check that there are no

soldiers or guards close by - she can't allow anyone to hear her speak to me. As if reading my thoughts, she offers me answers to my barrage of unspoken questions. "He has lost a lot of slaves recently … tens of thousands dead. Warden Horrell will replenish his numbers and he will allow her access to soldiers, supplies, and train routes."

If the slaves standing in the lines also nurtured the same spark of horror as I did, the degradation for them must have been unbelievable.

We know nothing of dignity. It is a basic human right we are never allowed to experience. We know, as soon as we receive the first strike of a fist, a baton, or a boot, where we stand in the world and how others see us. Today, I started to believe something new. There is only so much humiliation a person can take before they resist or fight back, even if they were bred to obey.

An epiphany punches me firmly in the stomach, sucking the air out of my lungs and trying to pull my body forward with pain. I have an idea why some have chosen to fight for us and why the war began in the first place. This abuse of power … this display of corruption, at its most primal level, is why people decided that change *had* to occur.

The man grabs a half dressed woman in her early-thirties and spins her around. He pokes at the protruding spine on her skin, pulls her short brown hair up and squeezes her shoulders. He rubs his chin before pushing the woman back in line. She lurches forwards, with the milligram of self-respect she still owns, and slowly puts her top on.

I see Warden Horrell and the man start talking with each other.

I wish I could hear them! I think but am too far away.

"Try not to stare!" says Adams.

Is the deal over? Have you two finished your human … your human transactions?

Warden Horrell waves over a group of security guards and the slaves are led away towards the awaiting trucks. The man smiles and laughs as he shakes hands with Warden Horrell.

The deal is done. A new alliance is formed ...

Warden Horrell escorts the man away from the cell blocks - they're heading in the direction of the administration complex. No doubt there will be elaborate feasts of succulent food and drink for him and his army this evening.

Where are you from? Which part of the world do you reside in ... that is also under attack?

My mind drifts. I do not travel to one of my usual places, though, and create a new scenario ... a new dream. I imagine myself walking through the gates of the administration complex and destroying everything inside. I obliterate buildings with a single look from my eyes, or a gentle wave of my hand.

"Eyes to the front," says Adams with more force. "You'll attract too much attention to us both!"

I pull my gaze away from the slaves as they climb in the back of the vehicles.

I wonder if any of them will survive the war? Will they ever return to Europa-Four?

"Do you trust me?" Adams doesn't look at me as she asks the question.

I need to see your eyes. I don't know why, but I know it will help me to answer you ...

I'm silent and indecisive for too long, so Adams stops walking near the side of my cell block building. There are no other military or security within hearing distance of us, and those in view are occupied with their own duties.

"My name is Serena. Everyone calls me Adams, though."

"I ... don't ... don't have a name ...," I say, almost whispering the words.

"I know ... but I want you to know mine. I want you to trust me ... even though it's a difficult concept for you."

I get my opportunity to examine Adams' eyes. They

seem genuine … almost familiar, yet in a manner I cannot explain to myself.

The sun disappears as a dense cloud rolls across the sky, covering everything and everyone in a sudden blanket of dark-grey. It fills me with a strong apprehension and changes my selfish disregard.

"Follow me, quickly." Adams turns left at the end of my cell block, heading in a direction I have never walked before.

"I … I'm not allowed," I say with a quivering tone. My feet stop due to instinct. If I continue, my trained and conditioned mind will scream in fear.

Adams stares at a steel door, a few metres ahead of us. The sign on the front delivers a clear and chilling message:

DO NOT ENTER. EUROPA-FOUR PERSONNEL ONLY.
UNAUTHORISED ENTRY WILL RESULT IN DEATH.

Adams grabs a pair of wrist restraints from her belt as she moves closer to me. "You have to trust me. You have to. This is a shortcut, that's all. We're using the security walkways to save us time. It might give us a chance to talk, although I can't promise anything."

My body refuses to move. I'm not sure I even want to. The clouds above thicken, mirroring my own fears with synchronised perfection.

"Put these on," says Adams. She holds the restraints out. "If we see any other guards, or soldiers, the fact you're wearing these will stop them from questioning you."

I step back. I do not understand Adams now. Her intentions, actions, and decisions are dragging me along with years of conditioned obedience.

"I know this is difficult for you, I do."

No you don't!

Adams looks around, hoping our actions haven't been

noticed. She holds out one hand as a gesture of trust and moves the restraints out of view. I know it's an attempt to calm me.

I hear a vehicle moving closer, its engine growling louder behind me. *Do it! You can't stay here and risk being seen!*

Adams look more nervous than I do, so, as my mind focuses on the courage of the woman on the train tracks, I step forward. My arms raise and I push my wrists together.

"Forgive me," whispers Adams, "and thank you."

••

After walking through the restricted door, Adams and I move for a couple of minutes down a well lit corridor. The bright fluorescent lights sting my eyes for some reason. No words pass between us until we reach a set of electronic doors.

My hands move over my mouth and I lower my voice. "Where are we?"

Adams doesn't answer. I don't know if she didn't hear me, or is deliberately ignoring my question. Either way, I don't repeat myself.

The doors slide open and we step inside a room with metal lockers running down the middle. The lights in the ceiling are dimmed, which helps my eyes to refocus. I can see uniforms hanging on rails at the right side of the room, shower cubicles ahead of me, and sofas to the left.

"There aren't any cameras in here. Warden Horrell respects, and is very serious about, the privacy of her female staff."

I nod. I can't think of anything to say because the room is like nothing I have seen before. I try to daydream about it, as if I am invisible, watching the guards preparing for duty.

Adams walks away with determined strides, moving

to her own agenda. I hear her opening a locker and rummaging about inside.

"Here," she says, reappearing with a backpack over her shoulder, "drink this while you have a chance. Sorry, it's only juice. I don't have anything else."

Adams unlocks my restraints and places a bottle in my hands. It's pure orange juice. I've seen it in the kitchen before, along with the other restricted ingredients.

"Hurry! We can't stay here very long." Adams grabs a new tunic, puts it in the backpack, then drinks from her own plastic bottle.

I open the lid and quench my thirst with large gulps. It tastes amazing, new, and fresh. I can almost feel the flavour radiating through my body. My stomach twinges, yet I continue. It has only ever experienced water before and isn't used to such natural sweetness.

"Ready?"

"Yes. Tha … thank you."

Adams takes my bottle back and locks the restraints over my wrists again. "Complete silence until we reach the outer doors. We're in dissecting corridors which run all over Europa-Four, cutting through the octants. They will take almost three-quarters of an hour off our journey to the Brunel line."

I never knew about this hidden network and it intrigues me in conflicting directions. It's an unexplored part of the city, an original and untouched map of information for me to study. It is also a nest for the armed rats, a secretive home for my violent masters, my … *my enemies? Have I decided to call them enemies now?*

Chapter eight

At the speed Adams marches, I'm provided with about fifteen minutes of time to study the bland corridors. The route isn't difficult to memorise, with only a couple of turns along the way.

"Be ready. There will be a platoon at the entrance to the station. I'll try to get us by them …," says Adams after we exit through another steel door. She doesn't look at me while speaking, "… but …"

"But what?" I ask. Again, I keep my voice quiet and put my hand over my lips to conceal them.

I notice Adams' knuckles flex slightly as the grip on her rifle tightens.

Is she scared of something?

"I only have so much authority here. The military outrank me and I can't disobey a direct order. It will create too much suspicion," she explains. Her voice wavers slightly. "The restraints, plus the fact I'll be telling them Warden Horrell gave me a direct order, should keep you out of danger."

What's worrying her?

I raise my hands and pretend to scratch at my face. "What's wrong? I know I'm not safe, but … there's more, isn't there? What aren't you telling me?"

Adams sighs and turns her head away from me. I know this behaviour because I've seen it many times before. I've used it myself on countless occasions in the past. It is to hide your face, your tears, and overwhelming emotions from another.

"Adams? Please?"

"A lot of …" Adams takes a deep breath. She still won't look me in the eyes, preferring to keep her head at a hidden angle. "… soldiers are beating or shooting slaves … for no reason. Well, there is a reason, a sick one. They're taking out their angers and fears without a second thought."

I want to speak. Adams should realise, and already know, I have lived with this brutality already for my entire life. Yes, it's probably magnified in its frequency, yet no different than yesterday, last week, or ten years ago.

As Adams and I walk underneath the large sculpture of branches and leaves, I notice how the twisted metal trees look different than they did this morning. The glistening metal has been replaced with a dull grey, due to the occasional dark cloud above, and it is almost alive, moving with the reflections of the uniforms passing by it.

It must be close to four o'clock now … too much has happened to me today in so few hours … to everyone here …

We arrive on the platform in silence and I see ten soldiers overseeing a group of slaves. They're moving wooden planks, tool chests, and steel bars towards the train tracks. Then, even though I try to keep my eyes away, I see something else … it's away to my left, on the floor by a concrete pillar. A grey and bloodstained sheet covers something … *someone …*

Adams walks over to the nearest soldier. He's average height, has black hair, brown eyes, and looks to be muscular under the uniform.

"Private Tsai, I need to transport this one down the tracks to the construction site. It's a direct order from Warden

Horrell," says Adams as we approach.

As Private Tsai turns to face us both, I see recent cuts on his hand and face. One glistens with a trickle of fresh blood.

Do I recognise you?

Usually, if I have encountered violence before, my mind will link it to the face of my attacker, often at a subconscious level. Anxiety and a jolt of fear will warn me if I need to be cautious. I feel calm … as calm as I can … as I stare at Private Tsai.

"What happened to you?" asks Adams as she points to the superficial wounds.

Tsai points the barrel of his rifle towards the bloodstained sheet. "One of the boys felt brave … or stupid. I dunno, I reckon everything today must have sent him over the edge. He grabbed a screwdriver and started swinging at me!"

And then he died ... fighting ...

"Stupid! Definitely stupid." Adams rolls her eyes with a slight laugh. "Anyway, this one, I need to get her to the site of the explosion."

"Understood. The carriage won't be back for ten minutes. Why don't you put her to work over there with the others?" suggests Tsai as he points to some of the slaves behind him.

"I'll drive her down in one of the Jeeps," states Adams. Her eyes look towards a group of vehicles parked nearby.

Private Tsai gives Adams a questioning glare and I panic.

Is this why she showed a moment of worry earlier? Has she created unnecessary suspicion?

"Warden Horrell wants her there as soon as possible …" Adams leans in, smiles and touches Tsai's shoulder. She blinks a few times and softens her eyes. "… And I'm starving! I'm going to grab my dinner in the temporary mess hall while I'm down there."

Tsai thinks about this for a second and then lets out a loud laugh. "Yeah, I hear ya! These new orders are messing with me as well. Do you know, I only had my lunch a couple of hours ago? I've been on duty since the explosion early this morning! I'd complain to the platoon leader ... but, I guess now isn't the right time. I'll end up yelled at because of these scum."

"Yeah, all this change ... because of *this* lot." Adams shoves her gun barrel in my back.

I stumble forwards and wince to add weight to her actions. I can hear Tsai laughing at me as I stumble away from him.

"Do you want me to take her out?" His nonchalant tone chills me. "Yeah, come on. It'll cheer me up to waste one of these filthy bitches!

I regain my balance and keep my eyes turned away from him. The sound of a holster unclipping sends my heartbeat to an unhealthy level. *Adams! Adams! Do something!*

"Turn around!"

NO! PLEASE ... NO!

Tsai moves forward with his gun pointing at me. I can feel the cold metal as it touches the back of my head.

"I said, turn ... AROUND!"

I cannot ignore my mind. I cannot ignore an order from a superior. My feet shuffle until the gun is pressed in the centre of my forehead. It feels as if my skin is splitting and the sweat is actually pouring blood.

Float away. Float away ... End your life in a peaceful and beautiful place ...

"Tsai! Tsai!" Adams stands next to him with her hand on one of his shoulders.

"What?" His eyes do not move, gripping at mine firmly. He wants to see the fear he has created.

Adams leans in and whispers an inaudible sentence. I wish I could hear it. I want to know what she is saying.

Tsai grins. He pushes me backwards with his gun, then turns to Adams and smiles.

"You … move!" orders Adams.

••

We reach a line of four military Jeeps, parked in painted bays on the left side of the train track.

"Get in that one." Adams sits me in the passenger seat, walks around to the driver's side, then starts the engine. Her voice is still commanding due to the ruse she wears like a second skin.

We head down the side of the train tracks and are soon clear of the platform and out of the dome. I breathe in the clean and unfiltered air. Europa-Four has developed a new aroma … one of smoke, oil, and sweat.

"We have a proper chance to talk. No cameras or audio surveillance until we reach the site of the explosion. What do you know already?" asks Adams. She slows the Jeep down as we reach a narrow gap between two maintenance buildings.

"How … how did you stop Private Tsai? Why didn't he kill me?"

Adams grits her teeth. "Don't worry about it. Answer my question, please?"

"Erm … nothing, really," I say, sensing Adams' urgency. I look out at the sea and find that it calms me immediately. "I've seen so much today but have actually learnt very little. I know the war began months ago. A boy told me this morning, after the explosion. M-532 … Do you … know him?"

Adams smiles, almost sarcastically. "Yeah, I know him."

He's one of them as well? He hides with us, like Adams does?

"Have you ever heard of Morse code?"

The question from Adams is unexpected and it causes me to pause for a few seconds. "Erm … what? Morse code? No. Is it for programming computers? Has it got something to do with the war?"

Adams lets out a small laugh. "Hundreds of years ago, it was created as a means of communication. It has been forgotten over the centuries … until now," she explains, allowing herself to smile with a tinge of superiority. I know it is aimed at Warden Horrell and others in power.

"I don't understand … I'm sorry," I say.

"It started on the same day, worldwide, at a predetermined time. Coded messages were passed between allied countries. Morse code is based on using dots and dashes to represent the alphabet. We use various punctuation marks because they can be, and were, added to e-mails or official communications. All the messages slipped through security systems, filters, and firewalls without detection. None of the software used has ever been programmed to search for it."

Adams smiles again. I know she is sharing in the triumph.

"The most important message was sent on the eleventh of June, at one-minute-past-one in the morning. Just one word. One piece of undetected code: dash-dot-dash-dash-dash-dot-dash-dash."

I stare at Adams, awaiting clarification. I probably look like a confused child to her, trying to understand intricate instructions.

Adams turns to me for a brief moment. "Now."

"Oh, so … erm … it was planned?" I ask. I had imagined many different beginnings to the war and none of them included such covert methods or actions. "It wasn't because of an invasion, or something like that?"

Adams shakes her head as we speed up. "I'll give you the short version … well, I'll try to. There are political, social, and humanitarian reasons which stretch back decades.

Government delegates have been meeting and discussing the state of the world over and over again, for years. Nothing ever came of it, unfortunately."

People wanted change for that long? Some of them do value our lives?

"Many countries around the world, plus smaller states and cities as well, they all began to condemn the slave trade. It had been abolished hundreds of years ago, before it resurfaced again in modern times. Many publicly apologised to their slaves and immediately shut down their fertilization clinics. Some cut off trade routes with neighbouring cities who didn't agree. Every act was designed to make a point and be heard by those in power. Does that make any sense to you?"

"I think so," I say and it is the truth. I am slowly understanding everything Adams is trying to explain to me.

"Once it became clear the constant meetings were a futile action, a date was agreed on and set with those in favour ... *the date*. On the eleventh of June, at one-minute-past-one, all the cities, countries, and regions involved declared it publicly. They were under new legislation and independent rule from the government. *That* was the day it began. *That* was the day when the world changed."

My heart jumps a few beats and I smile with a feeling I do not often experience when awake: elation. I recall my excitement on arriving back at the Brunel station earlier today, when it also happened. "It sounds ... sounds ... amazing ..."

"It was ... it is ... but it's also coming at a terrible price. The loss of life has been devastating."

"People like me? Slaves?"

"I'm sorry to say, yes. Most of the casualties are, but the military is suffering as well. I've seen small battalions wiped out in a single attack ..." Adams pauses to take a deep breath. "There's a lot of anger in this war and it has brought out the worst in humanity. Yes, hundreds of thousands of slaves have been freed and given equality in their cities, yet some still refuse to listen, like Warden Horrell. They won't accept the changes, they won't let go of the brutality, the power. Once you've tasted it, experienced it, the … sensation … it's too much to ignore. It's like an addiction."

I try to think of profound words, or any to add, but end up sitting in silence. I stare out to sea again … the endless expanse of water around me … it does not ease my inner fears as it did before. *Where do I fit in this war? What will happen to me if Warden Horrell never changes?*

Adams flicks a glance at me as a train carriage passes us on its way back to Europa-Four. "Do you do that a lot?"

My eyes frown with confusion.

"I've noticed it a couple of times now. You … daydream, especially when you're thinking about something," explains Adams.

"I … erm … use it, my imagination, I mean. It helps me."

"I understand," starts Adams. "You must have questions? Ask them now before we get to the construction site."

I have too many questions! I don't know which of them to ask first!

For a couple of seconds, I listen to the hum of the train, the Jeep's engine, and my own heartbeat. "Are there … erm … others, like you? Like the boy?"

"Yes, we're all over the world. The resistance web is strong yet invisible at the same time. We have a network of people who each lend their skills to winning this war. For example, all the paperwork I needed to transfer here had to be forged and, after the explosions this morning, I've been gathering information and delivering updates to those in the nearest city."

You have? You can talk to people outside of Europa-Four? "How?" I almost choke on the word because it flies out of my throat.

Adams takes one hand off the steering wheel and taps a finger on her watch. "Every detail I've gathered today has been passed to them ... and Warden Horrell has no idea it's happening!"

Every question breeds at least three more and I need to slow my thoughts down. My memory spins like a whirlpool as it picks out the young woman I saw this morning. "Did people from the city blow the tracks? I saw someone ... she crossed out her ink ..."

"It's called Aegis, and yes, we have many friends there."

Adams changes gear so that the Jeep travels along at a steady speed. "They blew it as a demonstration of their resources, and as a warning. They are cutting all ties to their enemies, Europa-Four now being one of them."

"Warden Horrell did the same. Someone told me that she ..." I stop talking to wipe my eyes, unaware I had started to cry. "... set off the explosives we all had to wear this morning. They were concealed in cuffs on our wrists."

I know I have many tears on my face. Talking with Adams about the true nature of the war is eating away at my soul, shredding hope with every second that passes.

"Yes, I'm afraid that is true. Europa-Four has enemies along the Equatorial line now. Warden Horrell acted in the same way as the people of Aegis did. She is cruel, as you know, and violence seems to drive her every action ... yet her mind is as sharp as a blade. She dissects every situation and every decision. Only success and victory are permitted."

"She's ... she's a monster!" I say with gritted teeth. I don't often feel this way - this passionate - yet it is overpowering me. My heart punches on my chest and I feel sweat on my face.

Adams slows the Jeep down so it is crawling along and follows a painted yellow line. I can see a few other vehicles parked ahead of us.

"I can't begin to imagine the life you've had ... and I

won't try to, ever … but we're nearly at the construction site. You need to pull yourself together, quickly!" Adams reaches a hand across and grips both of mine. I feel her warmth and genuine compassion.

I rub all the tears off my face and look at my protector, my new and only ally. A short amount of time with her has changed me in ways I can't yet understand.

"Thank you," I say. I try to pull my hand back because we are nearing the construction site. Other soldiers and guards may see the unwarranted and forbidden affection. It would mean instant death for us both. She won't let go of me, though. Adams is determined to hang on until her touch has calmed me down. The risks she is willing to take for me are living and breathing proof of the changing world. I can't, yet I wish to break down in tears again. Tears of joy, of hope, of belonging. I've never needed to feel these on my skin before.

"Follow orders, work hard, keep yourself invisible … be the perfect slave girl. War changes people, even those trained for it. They have never needed a reason to treat you with violent contempt before, have they? Have they?"

"No," I whisper as I grip back.

"That attitude has only been reinforced and magnified since this morning. It has become personal now, it has disrupted their lives … *you* have disrupted their lives. Every bullet, every explosion, it's now in front of their very eyes … and they're scared."

"We all are," I say in a meek tone as both our hands finally let go.

Chapter nine

It has changed so much here since this morning. I've been
working for a few hours now, carrying and stacking supplies.
The gap caused by the explosion has been almost fully
repaired by the military engineers. New wooden slats with
steel reinforcements, thick rails, and electricity towers are
back in place. Any debris from this morning's explosion has
been moved out of sight behind large tarpaulin sheets. I've
noticed quite a lot of dumper trucks transporting it away at a
steady rate.

*Is that because of us? Does Warden Horrell believe
we'll forget everything we saw, everything we felt ... simply
because it's hidden away?*

The security presence isn't as formidable as I thought
it would be. There are approximately twenty guards and
soldiers here, all commanded by a grey-eyed, six-eight tall,
and muscular man: Sergeant Major Hudson. His viciousness
is well known throughout Europa-Four, especially amongst
the slaves. He has grizzled features and scars across his
leathery skin, plus quite a lot of wrinkles, and cropped grey
hair. The first time I ever saw him, over six years ago, he
pulled out a handgun and put a bullet through the chest of a
slave ... *Because it was a hot day and his drink was served*

too warm.

After hours of carrying wood and steel bars from supply vehicles to the repaired area of the train tracks, I am allowed to stop and drink a cup of water. My stomach misses the delicious orange juice Adams allowed me to taste.

I keep staring down the Brunel line, hoping to see people or trucks. I know I want to see the young woman with glowing burgundy hair again. I want her to return and defy the soldiers as she did this morning.

The repairs are almost finished. I still don't understand why Warden Horrell needs this completed? Why would she waste effort on a route leading directly to her enemy?

As I think, I see Horrell's eyes in my memory, darting left and right as her mind ticked over. *Does she ... she plan to invade?*

Sergeant Major Hudson is only a few feet away from me and I avoid eye contact. He takes a look at his watch, then calls over two members of his platoon from a basic tent to his right. It's being used as the temporary command area.

"Yes, sir," they say in unison and both salute.

"It is now nineteen-hundred hours. We have approximately one-hour-and-fifteen minutes to get this completed before sunset. Warden Horrell wants the route open. It's imperative for the upcoming attack," he says, then turns to face the female soldier. "Get down there, Lieutenant Krazanski, and keep them all on schedule. Warden Horrell is preparing the carriage as we speak."

Attack? Carriage? Does Adams know about this? I swirl the crucial information around in my mind, unsure how to use it.

Sergeant Major Hudson's overconfidence has shown through, created through years of unchallenged power. He knows I am close by, as are a few others, but he doesn't see us as a threat.

What could a little slave girl do? Oh, I'll show you

what I can do!

Sergeant Major Hudson dismisses Lieutenant Krazanski and the other soldier, then walks away towards his command area. He sits down behind a portable table and snaps his fingers at another female slave. She runs over and quickly pours him a drink.

I can see sheets of paper in front of him on the table, yet none of the details printed on them are clear or visible. I cannot move closer. I am too scared to even contemplate the thought.

Do they show Warden Horrell's plans? I want to see them ... but there's no reason for me to be near him! I'll need to find Adams and tell her!

I finish drinking my water then pick up some more supplies for the repairs. My hands are shaking but I have to remember not to bring any attention on myself. I have to act as naturally as possible.

Where is she?

I walk down the side of the tracks for a couple of minutes, searching with unnoticeable movements of my head.

My heart leaps and I stifle a smile when I see Adams standing with two soldiers: one female, one male. They are talking with each other in a jovial tone, pointing up and down the Brunel line.

What do I do now? I must tell her what I overheard.

As I think of different ways to pass the information along to Adams, my body acts for me and my hands let go of the steel bars I'm carrying. They clatter to the floor and I feel nearby eyes staring at me with shock, pity, and contempt.

"Hey! Be careful with those!" growls the male soldier. He starts to walk towards me but Adams holds him back.

"Let go!" he shouts and stares at Adams' hand on his shoulder. "What do you think you're doing?"

Adams smiles in a playful manner. It reminds me of my horrific ordeal with Private Tsai.

"Take it easy, okay? Let me deal with this. I've already had to punish her today … Warden Horrell's direct orders. She obviously didn't learn her lesson the first time."

After a few seconds, the soldier relaxes. "Make sure she does!"

Adams marches towards me with her baton out. *What do I do? Are you going to hit me?*

"What's wrong with you, eh? It's a simple enough job!" Adams grabs my arm and spins me around. She runs her baton across my throat, as if to choke me. I can hear the soldiers laughing behind us.

"Stupid girl! You need to be more careful!" shouts Adams. Her voice suddenly lowers to a whisper and she moves her mouth next to my ear. "I'm going to walk you to the railing. Don't fight back."

I'm spun once more and I can see the soldiers now. Their faces have grins on them and they are openly laughing at me. They believe in the charade of my pain and public humiliation.

Adams turns again to conceal her face. "When we reach the railing, I'm going to push you … as if I'm about to throw you in the sea. That's when you talk to me. Be precise, and always keep your voice quiet."

I know none of her actions are real. I know Adams is saving me from real physical punishment. *She could even be saving my life … again …*

"Maybe it's too hot? Is the sun making you stupid? Yeah? How about I cool you down?"

The soldiers jeer Adams on, shouting at her. "She's gonna throw her in! She's gonna do it!"

Laughter follows from many directions. My imminent death is amusing to them.

My back hits the platform railing and I wince.

"Sorry," whispers Adams.

My chance to speak has arrived. I draw in a rushed breath and remember to whisper. "I overheard Sergeant

Major Hudson talking to some other soldiers. Warden Horrell wants the track completed so she can attack at sunset! I don't know how, but I know it has something to do with a train carriage! That's all I heard him say!"

Adams' pupils dilate as she places her hand on my stomach. "This is where I'm going to hit you."

I gulp in a sharp breath and close my eyes.

"Trust me! Drop to the floor and act injured," Adams whispers. She stands in front of me, then brings her baton down with a sharp whip. It stops mere centimetres from my skin as her grip loosens.

I slump off of the railing and curl my body forwards, adding a few loud coughs and choking sounds as well.

Adams bends down and grabs my face. "Stupid bitch!" she screams, then spits at the ground next to me. "Stay close to me. I'll give you new orders and try to keep you safe," she adds in a whisper.

"Get up! Go and stack that pile of wood over there. When you've finished, do the same to the steel bars … and don't drop anything this time!"

I get to my feet and nod my head, obeying her false orders. Adams' words to me in the Jeep return: '*Follow orders, work hard, keep yourself invisible … be the perfect slave girl.*'

••

After another bout of heavy lifting and moving supplies, sunset falls across the Brunel line. It brings with it a cooler atmosphere, which I welcome, yet also an unseen fear.

Is this it? Does Warden Horrell's plan start now? I think as more soldiers arrive in a military truck - at least twenty of them.

I can see Adams over by the left railing and have managed to stay close to her, as she wished me to.

A Jeep arrives and Warden Horrell steps out of the passenger seat. She walks to a stack of large tool trunks and climbs on top of them. "Attention!"

Everyone stops and turns to face her without a moment of hesitation.

"Operation Troy is now complete and will commence earlier than scheduled. Report to Sergeant Major Hudson immediately for your new orders!"

I watch Adams walk over to the command area as I carry a steel bar to a pile close to the railings. *What's Operation Troy?*

It takes a couple of minutes for Adams to walk back towards me. I see her face is different, as if it is now made of stone. It's set in an expression I haven't seen from her before, and don't wish to in the future either. She taps at the dial on her watch as well.

Something is wrong! She's sending a new message!

Adams holds her rifle with a tight grip as she nears me. Her head flicks to the side and nods towards my right, down the train line ... towards Aegis.

Is that a message for me? I don't understand what you're trying to tell me! I am disappointed with myself.

Adams eyes pierce through me as she repeats the actions. Her forefinger slips along by the trigger of her rifle this time, pointing in the same direction.

What do I do? I don't know what you want me to do!

Adams walks by me and stops next to another soldier. "Clever plan, eh?" she says.

The soldier turns to Adams and smiles. He nods his head as he pats her on the shoulder. "They won't know what hit 'em! Warden Horrell has been communicating with the leaders in Aegis this afternoon, playing their game, promising to release some of the slaves."

"Where are you based?" asks Adams. She speaks in a confident and loud tone, and I wonder if it's deliberate.

"I'm on the train," says the soldier as he pats his rifle with a sickening affection. "Once I arrive in Aegis, the fun begins!"

Adams turns to me for a brief moment and mouths a word. I can't quite see because of the dwindling light. It looks like ...

"RUN!" cries Adams. She pulls out a handgun and shoots the soldier in the leg. He falls to the ground and she grabs his rifle.

Run? Run where?

Adams turns around and opens fire in the direction of the command area. She moves herself behind a pile of steel bars with carefully paced side steps.

I dart to her side and kneel down for cover. I can hear bullets hitting the metal and it reminds me of batons running along my cell bars.

My thoughts scream at me, sounding like a different voice. Someone I do not recognise as myself. Someone full of tenacity and strength. *Stay low! Stay low! This pile of steel is keeping you alive!*.

"Take this! Just point it in their direction and pull the trigger!" shouts Adams with a frantic wave of her hand.

"What?"

A rifle lands next to me and glistens in the dwindling sunset. *Adams has given me a weapon?*

I realise I am now an unwilling, and unexpected, soldier, fighting by her side ...

Chapter ten

What do I do with a gun? I don't know how to shoot!

Adams fires a burst of bullets, lowers herself behind the steel, then grabs my shoulder. "When I give the word, we're both going to run behind those metal tool trunks. The ones further down the tracks. Okay?" she says as she grabs my face and turns it so my eyes meet with hers. She needs our actions linked together. She needs me to protect her.

I can't move! I can't breathe! My hands and feet are numb. I'm terrified and it has paralysed my body with incredible power.

"OKAY?" Adams kneels next to me and shouts her question. She knows I am retreating towards a state of shock and needs to halt it. "The others are on their way. We only need to hold our position for a few more minutes."

I am unable to speak and can do no more than stare at Adams' face. Her lips move and I'm trying to make sense of the noises coming out of her mouth. It's like I am underwater, or smothered in a thick liquid, and all the sounds around me are muffled.

I can't do it ... I don't know how to be brave ... I don't know how to do anything ...

A shadow moves behind Adams ... I can see it

getting closer to her … it wraps over the top and around the side of the steel bars … *What is that? NO! NO!*

A soldier stands only a few yards in front of me. He fires a handgun twice before I have even had a chance to process the situation in my already clouded and stunned mind.

Adams screams in pain as her leg flicks out. She falls at an awkward angle and her shoulder slams down on the steel bars.

Do something! Help her!

A rush of warmth coats my entire body and it feels as if I am suddenly being controlled by another. I am a puppet with strings pulling at my arms and legs. My arms move, my body moves … yet they are not my actions, my decisions.

I watch as my hand crawls forward to touch the rifle beside me. The cold metal tingles on my skin … it's now in my hands. I lift it up … my finger slides towards the trigger.

The soldier drops to the ground as Adams grips firmly around my wrist. Every sound magnifies with an eerie, lingering echo. The bullets, shouted orders, thudding boots … I hear them all now with a deafening clarity as they fly around my head.

"You … saved my life …"

"We need to get out of here!" I scream. My moment of forced courage is fading and I can feel the fear rising through me again, creeping across my skin and electrifying my veins.

Adams reloads her rifle with a swift move, despite her injured shoulder. "The … others … can you see them yet?" she asks, nodding down the train line.

See them?

I look down the train line. *Lights!*

"YES! I see them!" I cry. Dots of white light run across the platform, although I have no idea how far away they are. I imagine them as floating beacons of hope, rushing forward to cover us both in their protective glow.

Adams pushes herself to a crouching position. "Okay, the bullet to my shoulder is just a flesh wound but ... my leg ..."

She moves her body a few inches and lets out a pain fuelled scream.

I feel physically sick as it rings and stabs through my ears. Helpless. *WHAT DO I DO?!*

Adams drags herself backwards and growls through the agony. "There are more ... more tool trunks further down the track ... that we can use for cover," she stutters.

"I can't move!" I shout, urging my legs to feel once again.

"You can! You have to! Now, wait until I say, then fire a burst at the command area!" Adams does not give me any other choice but to listen and obey. I have always listened to the voice of authority, I'm familiar with its wicked tone, although this feels different to me somehow.

I grab the rifle with shaking hands and walk with crouched steps, keeping my body as low as possible. Adams is behind me firing her own weapon with more precise shots.

"NOW!"

I squeeze the trigger. The jolt from the gun purges my arms and hands of their nerves, shocking them awake, forcing them to fight. My feeble muscles tighten and react.

"Keep going!" shouts Adams. "We need to get behind those trunks and wait for the others!"

I shoot, take a deep breath, then move a few steps. My head spins around to check on Adams. I shoot again, breathe, move.

"Get down!" a male voice cries.

Who's that?

The lights are much brighter now, and I can hear new voices close by. *The others must have reached us!*

Adams touches my wrist. "We're safe. We're ... going to ... to be ..." She whispers the words as her body slumps to the ground. "... safe ..."

"What's wrong? Are you ... okay? Adams?
ADAMS?!"

NO!

Her eyes close. I jam my fingers on her neck and wait
as an agonising second passes.

SHE'S ALIVE!

My heart thumps with relief as I feel a pulse dancing
on my fingertips. The leg wound must have caused her to lose
too much blood. I don't want to worry about what I will do
with an unconscious body, so I push the thought away.

I'm joined by two new faces less than a second later.
They morph out of the lights and shadows: a young man and
a girl.

"We'll get her on the truck and back to the hospital.
Come on!"

The girl's voice sounds young to me ... too young.

They're the same age as me! And they fight?

I stand up, ready to run as the girl fires across the
train lines.

*Move out of the darkness. I want to see you. I want to
see your face and know you.*

I watch the muscles in her arms jump as each shot is
fired, admiring her skill and unwavering bravery.

Is this it? Is this the beginning of my freedom?

I turn. Adams is near a truck with the young man and
relief swims around my body.

A single gunshot cracks behind me. It is different
from all the others: louder and direct.

My face and neck are sprayed with a strange
substance. It feels hot and it clings to my skin.

What happened? My head spins around. I see a body
on the ground ... a young girl ... light-brown hair.

The world returns to its dull and silent void as I see
Warden Horrell running towards me with a gun in one hand
and a machete in the other.

NO! I need to get away ... She's going to ... to kill

me!

I run backwards and squeeze the trigger. My heel catches the ground, sending me flying. I land on my back with pain pounding at my chest and spine. I gasp in air because it hurts so much to breathe.

GET UP! GET UP!

Warden Horrell stands over me and her black eyes cut through the air. She doesn't speak a single word and her expression is not one of anger. The power to control her emotions this way is *more* horrifying to me.

I raise my rifle as Horrell swings her arm back, gripping her machete with an expert fist.

One shot is all I hear. One jolt of power is all I feel.

I close my eyes and wish to leave them like this forever, where it is dark and peaceful.

Would I be content to die now? I have been allowed to taste freedom ... just for a moment. Is that enough?

Voices crescendo all around me. Words run through the air alongside the smoke and bullets. I feel hands moving underneath my shoulders as I slip away to a numb world. It spreads up from my left arm, gripping my neck, squeezing at my throat.

As my body continues to lose all feeling, I do not know, or care, if I will ever return from this darkness.

Chapter eleven

I feel a warmth around me. No, it is much more powerful, more personal and intimate. I believe I am the pure source of this energy, its origin.

I try to breathe but my body resists the action. It is as if I don't need oxygen any longer.

What's wrong with my eyes?

I cannot see anything, although I believe my eyes are fully open. This is such a strange and unique experience. A void - infinite darkness - surrounds me. I'm unable to feel any singular part of my body, yet I do sense the warmth. It is inside me like blood and bone, flowing through me, swimming in and out of every pore across my skin. I imagine I am pulsing with an aura, and glowing with soothing heat.

Warden Horrell. Yes, I remember now. She stood over me before it all ended, before her machete cut through the air. What happened after the blade, though? Why can't I see it?

Is this ... death? Am I dead?

Chapter twelve

It is so quiet here. I feel safe. Always warm, so warm.
Is it possible to feel and think after death?

I do not understand, and I do not care to. I have no need for answers, or to even ask such questions. Nothing matters to me, except the energy which covets my skin. It holds an inexplicable and unrelenting desire, and we appear to be linked, as one.

Chapter thirteen

"How is she?"

Who's there? Where are you? I can't ... can't see you ... it's still so dark here. How can I hear you speak when I'm dead?

"No change."

"The arm?"

"Healing very well, Alden. As expected, from such a severe injury, there has been substantial tendon and muscle trauma, not to mention epidermal damage. The prosthetic has integrated to a satisfactory level. More than satisfactory in my personal opinion."

I don't recognise the voice of this man, Alden, or the woman either. I've never heard them speak before, I'm certain of it. They sound different. Their tone is much more gentle than I am familiar with. Nothing like the strict and domineering words of the security guards or soldiers.

I try to speak and urge my eyes to see these people. My body doesn't respond, though, and I remain in my strange world, my world after death. I am blind, suspended in my own body, listening to unknown voices.

Are they also dead? I remember M-197, an elderly male from block D. He told many stories about death, believing a place existed for the deceased to inhabit. He said, many times, you take the important memories and emotions of your life with you.

"She's in your hands, Doctor Higson. As you know, I am eager to meet this young woman … Daydream. Many of us are."

"I shall monitor her for another twenty-four hours. If, and I mean *if,* I am content with the results, I'll begin lowering the sedation levels." The woman speaks with authority and confidence. "The arm needs to remain in its rehabilitation casing, regardless of her physical state. The skin cells won't regenerate without assistance for another couple of days."

Why do they keep talking about my arm? What does Daydream mean? I do not understand.

Chapter fourteen

"I wonder what you're thinking about, Daydream?"

Adams, is that really you? Why did you call me Daydream? A man named Alden did the same.

"I hope you feel safe, wherever you are."

Are we both dead? My inner voice, it sounds so calm, too calm for such a morbid question.

If I can hear Adams' voice through this never-ending world, then she must have died as well. I tell myself this as pure truth. I didn't save her, protect her, keep her alive for just a few more seconds. We both exist in the infinite void now.

The blade. I remember how it glistened as Warden Horrell swung it towards me. I thought you had been rescued. I saw you by the truck with the young man.

I should experience guilt, sorrow, and failure, yet my body stays warm and unchanged, indifferent to any and all forces. My radiance is like a suit of armour.

Do I still possess a body? A physical form? This isn't how I imagined death. I thought it would be final. Ultimate. Not like this. There is no purpose here. No beginning and no end.

"You need to come back. You need to open your eyes and start moving."

I ignore Adams' words and continue with my own questions. *How long have I ... we ... been in the darkness for? Can you hear me? Is this how we will communicate now, with our thoughts?*

"Wherever you are, I'll be there with you. Is that okay? Can I join you?" asks Adams. Her caring voice appears to be close and distant in the same moment.

Chapter fifteen

"Can I join you?"

Blurred light floods around me as colours punch at my strained eyes. I am suddenly thrown down a spiralling tunnel, as if flying at an imaginable speed. I sense the thought of nausea but it disappears as I concentrate on my returning sight.

"Can I join you, please?"

My body stops. A tidal wave of shapes and forms pour around me, yet I am untouched, standing immune.

I know this place. I'm in the orchards of Octant two. Is this the next part of death, revisiting familiar places? It would make sense for my imagination in life to mould my journey now. M-197 spoke the truth.

I look at my body. It's the first time I've seen it since the train tracks. The first time since Warden Horrell.

My skin looks new, without scars or bruises, and most of my movements are fluid, almost poetic. My left arm is the exception, unable to follow the rules or carry the newly formed, crisp, detailed lines. It is indistinct, vague, and completely numb.

"How does it feel? Your arm?"

"Adams!"

I don't know how or why she appeared next to me. Seeing her causes me to feel more than warmth for the first time in …

How long did I spend in the dark? How long was I frozen in time? I don't care for a reply. Hours, days, and weeks - time itself - seems irrelevant to me. Trivial and unnecessary.

I move to grab Adams in a tight embrace, wanting nothing more than to hold her. My muscles scream in pain and betray me. They feel weak, so I end up walking the few steps towards her in a stuttered fashion.

You're skin is so warm, like mine. Do you feel the same as I do?

I hold Adams, again ignoring any concept of time, as the sun drenches us both. The flickering shadows which beam through the leaves and branches dance across our faces, the grass, and the tree trunks. I have never known a sense of happiness and freedom such as this one.

I don't want to let go! I want to keep you close to me. You make me feel safe.

Adams moves back a step as she takes a loud bite out of a green apple. She holds one in the palm of her other hand for me. "Do you want it, Daydream?"

"Daydream? Why do I keep hearing that word?" I ask.

Adams stares at the sky and her face glows in the sunshine. "You needed a new name. You're not a slave now, so your identifier is useless."

I suppose that is true. Death freed me.

"I hope you like it. I chose it for you," says Adams.

I smile, take the succulent looking fruit, then roll it in my hand. The sun bounces off of its smooth peel. "Thank you," I say, realising how hungry I am. My stomach flutters at the notion of food.

Adams doesn't resent me for failing to protect her? I can't sense any blame in her voice or behaviour.

I don't dwell on my thoughts and sink my teeth into the apple. My face winces. *It tastes like ... blood!*

"Are you okay? What's wrong?" asks Adams. She moves closer and holds my hand with a comforting strength.

I spit the piece of apple out on the ground and run my tongue across my teeth. It feels as if there is something still in my mouth. It has an odour and texture which reminds me of plastic tubing, much like those which spread out of the harvesting machines in the hospital. They are grotesque, as is their duty, like mechanical and electrical tentacles.

I feel ... cold? I've felt warm for so long. What's happening to me?

My spine tingles with negative thoughts as I pick up the scent of antiseptic. The blood thickens as it mixes with a sterile and bitter flavour. My work in the research laboratories also brought this atmosphere with it.

I turn to speak, to find the comfort I need so much right now. "Adams? ADAMS! Where are you?"

I spin around, searching through the trees and bushes in the orchard as a dark cloud covers the sun.

I'm alone. Why did she leave me here?

Chapter sixteen

The sun grows in the sky, ripping its way through the thick clouds. It's bright, too bright, and I shut my eyes as the orchard - the entire world - is consumed by a white coat of heat and light.

My throat stings and tightens. I can feel it being scratched and cut as I try to breathe once again. I have to now. I need to fill my lungs with clean air.

My stomach clenches and I grit my teeth together with force and pain. The taste of blood returns, more potent than before, coating my tongue and lips.

Did Adams bring me here to punish me? Is this because I failed her? I'm sorry! Adams, I'm so sorry ... I tried!

Chapter seventeen

"What? I don't understand you! What are you trying to say?" begs Adams. Her voice is desperate, loud, and confused. "Breathe through your nose and try to relax. Please, just stay calm!"

I feel a strong grip coil around my wrist. *I don't like this place! It's different, too real. It's cold and painful. Adams! Help me!*

Vague lights flash and move around the small space I now exist in, merging with my thoughts and Adams' voice. It's small and enclosed, unlike the dark void.

"Listen to me, listen." Another joins us and I feel added pressure on my arms and shoulders.

I recognise this other woman. She spoke in the darkness. *You're a doctor ... you spoke to Alden.*

"Don't be afraid. You can trust her. She is here to help, I promise."

"Adams!" My word sounds slurred, somehow hindered and blocked.

"She's one of us!"

One of us. One of them. Such a simple split through the world.

"Count to ten! Come on, Daydream! Breathe deeply,

through your nose if you can, and listen to my voice. One …
two …"

Adams is close to me. I can see the shape of her face,
its edges are outlined with a feathered light.

Three … four …

"Five … six … seven. The injection will help you to
relax, that's all it's for."

*Eight. Injection? I don't feel anything … nine … t …
ten …*

"I'll begin the extubation procedure. Hold her hand,
please, Adams."

A pressure follows on my chest and I cough with all
the air I've managed to pull inside my lungs. My throat rips,
shreds, and stings again as my head rolls to the side. I retch,
then groan because the actions strain my stomach muscles
and ribs.

*What's wrong with me? Where am I now? I miss the
warmth on my skin.*

"Okay, I'm done," says Doctor Higson. "She will be
fine, just give her a minute or two for the relaxant to stabilise.
I need to contact Alden immediately and update him."

"I'll stay with her. Thank you," says Adams.

I can hear the relief in her tone and sense an immense
weight of frustration drifting away, dragged out of the room
by Doctor Higson.

*It's quiet again, peaceful. I enjoy this. I cannot stand
the noise and lights at the moment.*

I lie still with my eyes closed, trying to adapt to my
new world. First, the darkness and warmth, then, the pain and
punishment endured in the orchard. Now, I can't yet explain
this experience, or understand it. I *want* to, though, which is
different. I care to understand once again. I need reasons and
must have answers to my questions.

"I'm so sorry, Adams …" I mumble because my
throat aches with every word, and fresh blood swims inside
my mouth.

A hand touches my face, as if it is nothing more than a soft piece of silk floating around me.

"Sorry? Why are you sorry?"

"We ... died. I couldn't save you," I say with a cracked voice.

The hand runs down my cheek with an added dose of strength. Then, I feel something land on my right arm.

A drop of water?

I open my eyes. The world is bright again and too full of screaming colours. They stab at my eyes and forehead, pounding from the inside like tiny claws and fists.

Focus. Take it slowly.

I blink a few times and concentrate on the large blur in front of me. *Adams? I'm trying to see you, I'm trying to find you!*

Her eyes clarify first, then her mouth. It has an unusual smile on it, concerned and partly forced, contradicting the intended emotion.

I see a few sparkles of white light as I return to Adams' eyes. They move down across her skin. It's the light reflecting off of her tears.

Why are you crying?

I clear my throat, preparing it for the expected onset of pain. "Adams," I say. My voice rasps and stutters with unnecessary breaths. "Why are you crying? Is it my fault? Because I ... I couldn't save us?"

Adams' hair strikes into view. Perfect strands, flowing lines without distortions. She looks beautiful, so alive and vibrant.

"No ... no!" Adams sounds upset. "We're not dead, Daydream. We're alive! You're in a hospital in Aegis."

Alive?

I can't think of anything to say. I watch more tears flow down Adams' face as my own escape the outer corners of my eyes. My muscles tense once again, however, this time it is caused by excitement.

What? Is this another part of death? Will I be taunted with false hopes now?

"After the fight on the train tracks, we returned here to reevaluate our position. You've been sedated for a little under a week."

I hear Adams. I hear her words. My mind resists them all, though, caught between acceptance and denial. Part of me believes this is another step in my journey after death. I'm to endure a new lesson brought with me from the living world.

"We survived? We're safe?" I ask, unsure if I will believe the response.

"Yes, we survived, yes!" Adams nods her head while she wipes her eyes dry. A pause follows as her attention drifts to the window on my right side. "Safety, I'm afraid to say, is still an ideal we all strive for. The war isn't over."

I stare towards the window as well, trying to imagine the world outside. *We're alive? ... I'm alive ...*

Chapter eighteen

An incredible surge of disbelief, shock, *and* euphoria pulses through me. It is a conflicting recipe which forces me to shake and feel physically ill, despite the positive of the moment.

I'm alive ...

My eyes dart around the room, their sharp and erratic movements matching those of my thumping heartbeat.

Adams said I was in a hospital.

I scan vague details of the room with rapid, blurred, glances, and touch the cold metal of the bed rails with my bare feet.

I can see again and feel the world around my body. The darkness of the void has gone.

I look at the window once more. Rays of streaming light cut through the half-open blinds like blades of ethereal gold. I want to see the free world and explore Aegis.

My thoughts are naïve and blinded, even arrogant. They know I am surrounded by machines, used to monitor my physical state, and they feel the atrophy in my muscles. It clings to my entire body like a layer of weighted skin. They still push me to move, to sit up, to absorb myself in the moment.

Wha ... what's wrong with me?

My left arm fires a stab of pain through my shoulder and neck. I focus my attention, this time specific and lucid, towards the pain.

Why is my arm inside a ... machine?

I freeze with panic, staring at the light-grey, cylindrical, apparatus.

It runs from my bicep to my knuckles, clamping my limb so movement is almost impossible. The circumference - just over an inch of metal and plastic - has bolts running through it.

"It will be okay, Daydream. Stay calm." Adams grabs my right hand as she sits on the bed. Her voice is forceful and she deliberately puts her face in my eyeline in an attempt to redirect my attention.

I take a few deep breaths as my body resists. I tense my muscles and move my fingers - just visible, extending from the open end of the machine. The touch screen on top of it displays animated graphs and long streams of numbers.

I watch for a few seconds, almost hypnotised, however, I cannot make any sense of the readouts.

"Adams?!"

I have a glass of water thrust in my right hand as a soothing palm runs down my face.

"Listen to me. Listen! It's fine, okay. Doctor Higson will be back soon to explain what happened," snaps Adams. She looks at the door in the room, almost hoping her words will come true.

My memory struggles to replay the chaos which occurred on the train tracks in Europa-Four. The gunshots and shouting voices, mixed with my own fears, have all created an uneven recognition.

I had a gun. I fired it, protected Adams. Others came to help us.

"How? What happened?" I ask, even though I already know the answer.

The blade!

Adams' eyes answer first. Then, she utters the single word, the feared name, which I am expecting. "Horrell."

I remember pulling the trigger on my rifle. I fired it at Horrell. I fired as the blade flew towards me.

"Can I see? Please?"

Adams is reluctant to answer, or even acknowledge my request.

"Please!" I repeat. This time, I lock with her eyes so she can't avoid the situation. "I have to see!"

Adams sighs as she pushes the glass of water towards my lips. She closes her eyes for a brief moment, then, her hand reaches across and taps at the touch screen on top of the machine.

While I was in the darkness ... I heard the voices! They spoke about my arm!

I think of my unconscious dream about the orchard in Octant two. Every part of my body looked fresh and unharmed, except for my left arm. It was nothing more than a limp blur. An alien limb I could not sense, use, or control.

"It can't be fully removed, you understand? It is regenerating your skin tissue. I can separate it enough, though, so you can see."

Adams' fingers pause with hesitation. "It may ... scare you at first. Try to stay calm, don't make any sudden movements, and resist the urge to touch your skin."

Scare me?

I nod my head and concentrate. Adams' words are not registering inside my mind, so I shout at myself to listen and heed the important instructions. The world, my whole world, is now constricted to nothing more than my arm and its surgical casing.

The machine beeps a couple of times. I feel its grip lessen, similar to the blood pressure cuffs used to monitor all the females during harvesting.

Don't be afraid ... Don't be afraid!

I did not care for time in the void, or the orchard, yet as I wait with deep breaths, every second evolves to twenty.

I feel a slight vibration in my upper arm as the top half of the machine moves on unseen hinges. It lifts open with a gentle, mechanical, sound to reveal my left arm.

No ...

Chapter nineteen

A couple of weeks after I was inked with my fourteenth age marker, I injured my leg in the steel mills. While being transported across the store room, a small container full of chain links fell from its mechanized pallet. It crashed down on my right knee, cut a deep slice in my shin, and I fell to the ground. My entire leg was covered in blood and I couldn't move. The pain and severe cut were not my first worries, though, my inability to tidy up my mistake and return to work were. An idle slave is a target. An incompetent slave needs to be reminded of the rules.

NO!

The guards and work supervisors blamed me for the accident, and punished me with strikes from their batons, a few stinging slaps around the face, and kicks to my bleeding leg with their steel toe capped boots.

My ... my arm ...

I recall the appalling beating, allowing my mind to take me back. At the time, it was the worst injury - and example of the violent laws which governed me - I had ever experienced.

Horrell ... she ... took my arm!

My eyes, covered in a layer of tears, flick to the long

scar on my shin. If I stare at it long enough, if I believe with all my heart, it might remain as the most destructive mark on my body.

Instead of skin, I see a translucent substance, a living mesh. It has darker, more toned, areas running through it, like the crawling roots of a plant. Underneath, the light in the room finds metal, bolts, and clusters of wires. An electromechanical creation, attached to the bones above my elbow.

I stretch my fingers without thought. It's instinctive, created by pure shock and a savage, infinite, dread. The metal rods rotate, extend, and pivot accordingly, matching the actions of the missing bones, muscles, and tendons.

I can't feel it! Why can't I feel anything!

I drop my glass of water and grip Adams' hand as I take in enormous lungfuls of air, fearing unconsciousness. My eyesight blurs and I let disturbing thoughts enter my already sickened mind.

Get it off me! I don't want it! I DON'T WANT IT!

I grip Adams' hand even tighter, then ease up a second later. The thought of causing her any pain helps to pacify my impulses towards self mutilation.

"I'm so sorry," says Adams. "Don't be afraid. Try and stay calm. Doctor Higson told me there would be unpredictable reactions when you regained consciousness."

Adams' words are nothing but a muffled block of sounds. I can't move my eyes away to look at her either.

"I put you in terrible danger out there. I - I shouldn't have. This might not have happened."

These words, especially their apologetic and guilty intention, are clear to me. *No! I don't blame you for this. I don't!*

"You can't think like that! Please! Warden Horrell did this to me, not you!" I grit my teeth in anger and tense my muscles, despite their weakness.

I recoil for a split second, not recognising my own

inner strength. My throat tightens and burns because of my raised voice.

"Let me find Doctor Higson. She can explain everything to you about the surgery." Adams stands up and heads for the door. She has an urgency to her movement and body language. "I may not be a physician, but I know you'll recover from this. Trust me, okay?"

I nod and force a smile as Adams leaves, watching her shadow spread like paint across the floor outside my room.

"Wait!" I try to call out.

I wanted to know about Warden Horrell! Is she alive? Is she still in Europa-Four?

I stare with a sickening infatuation at my mechanical limb. The rods inch forward as my fingers move. For strange reasons, ones I cannot explain, I begin to see a beauty in the engineered accuracy.

Can I ... lift it? The machine doesn't look heavy.

With a thousand other questions sparking like embers floating away from a fire, I move my arm in apprehensive steps. A centimetre of motion, rest and check for pain, then another. I feel incomplete, because of the loss of sensation, despite knowing I am controlling the false appendage. I expect to feel *something.*

After lifting it another few centimetres, I'm surprised at how natural the experience is. There is a dull ache over my shoulder and upper arm, where my real skin is scarred and still healing.

"Hi," says a quiet voice.

I look towards the open door to see a few locks of brown hair poking out beside the frame. The tight curls loop and swirl three-and-a-half feet off the ground.

"Erm ... hello?"

"Hi," repeats the voice.

The single word carries a pitch and innocence. My curious imagination links it to that of a young girl. It is also the first time I've allowed the world to extend beyond this room, beyond my own, sometimes selfish, mindset. After realising I was still alive, and learning of my injury, I have let my thoughts centre on myself and nothing else.

Is she a patient here? Someone so young has been injured in the war?

"You - you can come in, if you want to? My ... erm ... my name is ..." I cough to clear my throat and regain my voice, then pause as I focus on my arm.

Since my memories began, my name, my inked numbers, have always been there.

My name is ...

My heart pumps with accelerated vigour.

... Daydream.

The cruel and sadistic Warden Horrell took my arm from me, yet she took something else at the same time.

I study the tendrils of regenerated skin. Newer strands are pure white, others match my own perfectly. This time, I do not see the mechanics, I do not see the results of Horrell's blade.

I do not see F-918.

"My name is Daydream," I say with confidence. "What's yours?"

There is no answer as I watch the brown hair move a couple of inches closer towards the doorway. Light-brown skin sneaks into view as well from the girl's face, then darts away.

"You don't have to be shy," I whisper.

I hear a tapping noise on the floor as the girl pokes a curious eye in my direction. I notice it is golden-brown in colour, however, my attention is drawn to the brace around her leg. It taps a few more times as she regains her balance, ensuring she is somewhat hidden.

There are four straps attached to the thick metal bars on either side of her lower leg.

"Did you hurt yourself?"

"Okay. Bye!"

The girl disappears and I listen to the tapping move away down the corridor. She is trying to run, even though the use of her leg is impaired. I smile at her innocence and behaviour, so different to the petrified faces I am used to.

When will I be allowed to leave here? I want to see outside, to walk freely through Aegis.

My eyes return to my arm, to the blank patch of skin which used to control me. I think of the explosion on the train tracks and how I cried on seeing the young woman cross out her identifier. Now, I have been granted freedom. I am no longer a slave.

A shout from outside travels through the window, catching my attention. It's not clear so I can't make out the word.

Is something happening?

I let panic grab me for a second, remembering the war isn't over. It is right now, surrounding the entire world.

A cheer erupts. I hear laughter. Excited voices mingling with each other.

It sounds like ... like ...

My eyes fill with tears as the chant crescendos and synchronises. It sounds as if hundreds of people are calling out as one, sending a pulse of warmth to spread throughout my body.

One word is being repeated.

One word.

Daydream.

PART I: THE END

117

Hello, reader, and thank you :)
I hope you enjoyed this dystopian tale. I have to admit, it was an extremely intense story to work on, and I have more to complete in the near future. Female 918, or *Daydream,* as she is now known, has more to tell us.

On the following pages, I have included a sample chapter from *My Long Journey to Sincerity,* another dystopian novel of mine. It introduces us to Elana Mayne, one of my favourite characters … well, to be honest, I love all my characters equally ;)

Thank you once again,

Jason

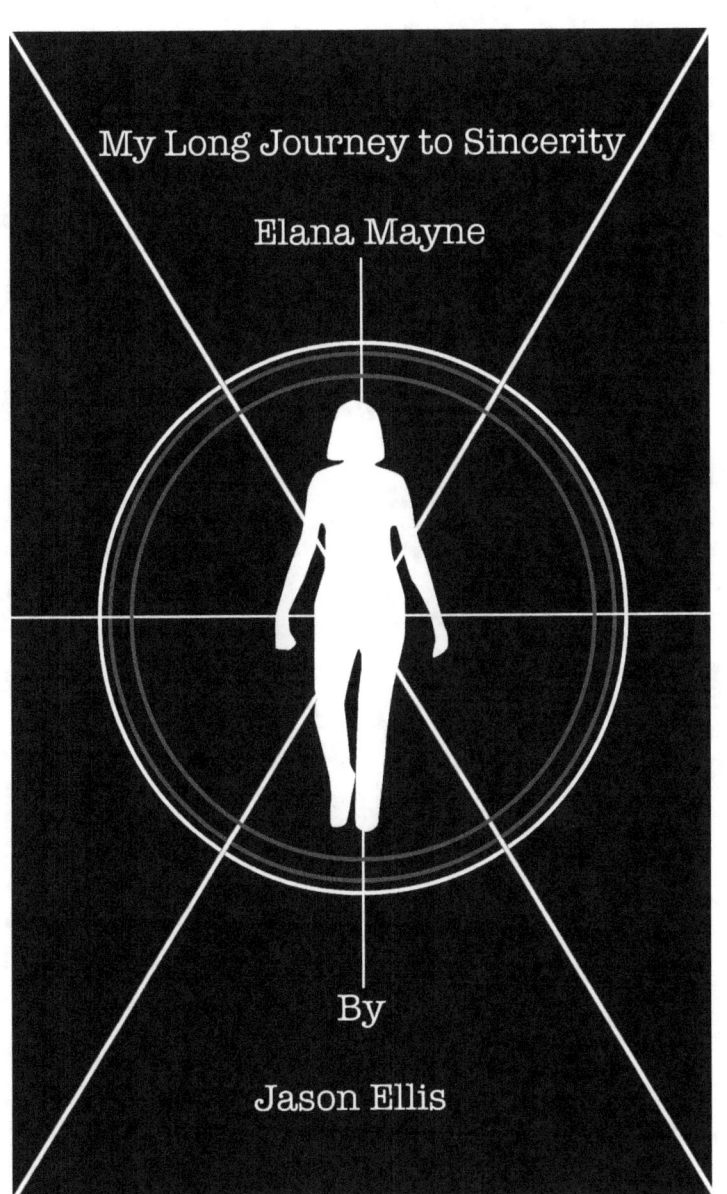

My Long Journey to Sincerity

Elana Mayne

By

Jason Ellis

My Long Journey To Sincerity

..

Elana Mayne

by

Jason Ellis

My Long Journey To Sincerity

••

Elana Mayne

Published by JTT Publishing

ISBN 13: 978-1-906529-57-4

Dedication

For my family. I write, you all make me smile and laugh. I talk for hours about plots, characters and oh-my-goodness-that-is-so-amazing twists. "Sounds great," you say. ;)
For my friends.
For all the readers.
I have to mention Happy Days because of the daily laughs, boulders … and Queen Bee arenas!
Cenx and Redigit - Mr. and Mrs Terraria. When is the author NPC being added? :)
And Jessica Heeren. A unicorn, sewing, and a bald cat. Even with my imagination, that wasn't a dream! It really happened :)

A message from the author.

Some time ago, I began working with Louise Sargent. We planned to publish a book together, based around a main character with Myalgic Encephalopathy (ME), and Chronic Fatigue Syndrome (CFS).
Unfortunately, I never managed to complete the story. I couldn't seem to do it justice (I'm extremely harsh with self-criticism) and writer's block soon kicked in as well.
Louise has suffered with M.E., for many years and launched M.E. Support to raise awareness.

Louise kept in touch - she remembered to post Christmas cards, I forgot most years … I'm terrible, sorry, Louise ;)
Recently, we started talking about the book again. As I was completing this title, I had the idea to aid Louise's work a slightly different way. I shall now be donating a percentage of royalties from the sales of this book to help Louise, the volunteer base, and her support websites:
www.mesupport.co.uk
www.facebook.com/MESupportUK

••

M.E. Support was founded in 2001, and is one of the leading websites on Myalgic Encephalomyelitis, providing information, advice and support.

Chapter one

"Stop! Put your hands out to the side!"

What's happening?!

The unexpected voice startles me as it booms through the hallways of the college building, echoing off the blank walls.

My fear spikes as I see a couple of Community Guards standing in the middle of the corridor, pointing their weapons directly at my head. I move my arms up as instructed, then freeze. The barrels of the handguns are two feet away at the most, staring me down like silver eyes in the moonlight.

The familiar black uniforms confront me as if stone statues have punched out from the ground: boots, khaki trousers and a thick jacket. I know that others are behind me as well, forming an impenetrable barrier. I can hear thick rubber soles thudding on the plastic floor tiles as they manoeuvre to set positions. I dare not move to check if my assumptions are correct.

"Keep your hands up! Stay exactly where you are!" orders one of the guards.

I tense every muscle, willing myself to comply, although my body is shaking and I'm finding it difficult to stand still. It is an impossible situation.

One of the guards steps forward, never letting his aim falter. I can't see his face - all guards wear a helmet with tinted visors, regardless of their division. It has the letters *CG* embossed on it in a dark red colour, surrounded by a circle.

A gloved hand reaches towards one of the many equipment pockets attached to the belt around his waist. Without lowering his weapon, or moving it by even a single centimetre, he pulls out a small metallic device. It beeps once before he runs it along my limbs and body, seemingly paying particular attention to my hands. Then, he holds it close to one of my blue eyes, recording and checking the retina.

As I stand here, waiting for the scan to finish its cycle, all I can do is wonder what he could possibly be looking for - no crimes, abstract or physical, have been committed.

I've done nothing wrong!

"She is clean! Stand down!"

The guns lower, yet are not holstered.

"Elana Mayne, yes?"

It is so difficult to speak clearly, yet the words make their way out of my dry throat, somehow. "Ye … yes … I am Elana Mayne."

"Slowly, and without any sudden movements, reach for your identification card," says the guard. He speaks with determination and clarity.

I lower my right hand down to the waist of my trousers and unclip the laminated card, holding it out at arms length. My hand is visibly trembling and I am having trouble fighting it off.

The Community Guard takes it and uses the same metallic device to scan the information. "Have you seen anyone else in the college library today?" he asks while waiting for my identification to upload and record.

"No, I was just here to …"

An arrogant and authoritative hand shoots up, stopping me from continuing the sentence. Everything after the word 'no' is irrelevant information as far as he is concerned. "Did you speak to anybody?"

"No, I've only just arrived," I answer, keeping my words short and to the point.

Another of the guards walks forward, carrying a thick book. She holds it up so close to my face that I have to blink in order to refocus my eyesight.

"You were reading this book during the past week, yes?" she asks. "We have you on surveillance, so don't even try to deny it."

I gently nod in agreement. *If she already knows, why bother to ask me? And why are they so interested in the books I've been reading?*

"Have you seen anybody else reading this book recently?"

"No."

"Did you notice anything different about it? Did you alter this book in any manner?"

"Erm ... no ... I didn't do that! I don't understand!"

I'm pleading my replies now, hoping for the situation to be over. I'm angry with myself as well because I shouldn't hesitate when answering their questions. I know such actions are considered as a weakness of character, possibly brought on by guilt. That's how the guards surrounding me could see it. They are trained to see it that way.

Silence follows for half a minute, although it feels a lot longer for me. I can hear the thumping heart in my chest as the seconds tick by and sense the visored eyes all pointing at my face. The world is now a paradox for me: a speeding heartbeat yet time has slowed down.

"You may leave, Elana Mayne," says the guard as he returns the ID card back to me.

With no further words, or hint of an explanation, the

group of Community Guards march off through the corridors of the college library.

I may be physically and mentally shaken by all of this, yet I'm accepting of the situation, too. After all, this is normality. This is life for me ... for everyone. The decisions and actions of Central Government, and its various departments, are not to be questioned. *'Know that we are always working for you. We make the decisions, so you don't have to. We make the laws to ensure that you are always safe. Trust our judgement.'*

The hallways return to complete silence once more.

Calm down ... pull yourself together! You have to! The interrogation is soon ...

••

I sit at a desk in one of the side rooms that are built off of the main library auditorium, studying the thick textbook in front of me: *Scientific Principles in post virus society, by E. Volf; CGSc. Central Government approved author, #131.* I have already passed the examination, so this is more of a recap session, *and* a welcome distraction.

The imminent presentation to designated university representatives needs to be perfect. It is the chance - the *only* chance - to promote my abilities, intellect, and character. The selection process is a daunting experience, yet also an important and crucial rite of passage, compulsory for all sixteen year old students, signalling the transition on their path to adulthood. It is officially titled as the *day of progression.* The title that all teenagers whisper, yet never dare to voice out loud - *The interrogation.* Some have spoken of how they were questioned for hours, yet some for a much shorter time. The anticipation has become more frightening than the actual event for a lot of people.

My entire future - the future of all the sixteen year old

4

students in *all* the communities - depends on the grades we have received so far in academic testing. They determine which Central Government department may choose us for their training initiatives. Our entire lives will be planned, waiting for us to obediently follow, based on this one meeting.

After a few more minutes of reading, I check the digital clock on the wall, seeing it is 10:31. I need to leave the college library straight away and travel to my interview in the centre of the Community Zone. Fortunately, as the poster on the wall next to me states - *The wise and caring Central Government always keep the public transport systems running smoothly and efficiently.*

It isn't a difficult task in all honesty - only two methods and routes exist: trams either continuously hum around the square perimeter, or cut through it, delivering people to their homes, places of work and education, or trains venture further afield, to another community. The railway network connects the entire globe, with only some long distances - those across the oceans - carried out by an automotive or water-craft service. All air travel is restricted to military personnel or selected members of the government.

"If you don't feel ready now, you never will," I mutter to myself. "Come on, get up. Let's go!" I add, just for a push of confidence.

I stand up, take the textbook back to its shelf, then head for the exit. On the way, I visit the toilets so I can check my reflection in one of the wall mirrors. I want to make sure my appearance isn't at fault. The interrogation will be tainted if I turn up looking unkempt.

Hair is neat. Fingernails clean and filed ... and my clothes are fine, I think as I look down at my permitted outfit, all Central Government issue: a white tunic, black trousers, and a pair of laced plimsolls in grey. I have three more of all these items back at my living quarters. They are delivered weekly to all the residents, and the worn clothes are taken away at the same time for cleaning. Yet another example of the efficient world I live in.

The college library looks like every other building in the Essex Community Safe Zone, every other building in all the Safe Zones if the truth be told. They are grey and bland ... sterile and fortified. Smooth concrete walls are always set at perfect right angles, creating an inner network of corridors that mark out the different library areas. The inside of the main college building is exactly the same, as are the schools, and the majority of housing. A design must have been agreed upon and then repeated and resized as many times as the architects decided was necessary. Build ... stack ... repeat.

A few minutes later I walk through the steel doors of the South wing, stepping outside to the college train station. I see two Community Guards nearby and, for a few nervous seconds, expect them to turn and aim their guns at me, as they did earlier. *They're just on a normal patrol ... nothing else ... just a normal patrol ...*

Growing up in a safe zone is a double-edged sword most of the time. I've seen violence and ... *justice,* carried out swiftly and with cruel precision. It still sickens and terrifies me ... *everyone.* The price of security is worth paying, though, if it keeps danger, trouble - or possibly worse - out of the communities. These are the only habitable areas created by Central Government, varying in size and number of residents. Some are entire countries from the old world, others mere pockets of society, such as the one I live in. The rest of the planet is either designated as a Wild Zone - they house many of the dangerous animals of the world, those which did not succumb to extinction when the virus hit - or an Inhabitable Zone. These are dangerous, contaminated areas. People who have tested positive for the virus are exiled there. Even those with a possibility of infection, or showing symptoms such as erratic thoughts or behaviour; *fifty-fifties* as they are colloquially known, are sent to such horrific places. As far as I know, these unfortunate individuals either die soon from the infection, or manage a few years of prolonged existence, scavenging through the old world, surviving by any means possible.

Today is a warm Friday in the middle of May and the late spring sun is shining brightly, despite a few clouds floating across the sky. They are like random dabs of white paint, smudged to near transparency. My straight black hair, cut a couple of inches above my shoulders, occasionally blows across my face because of the mild and cooling breeze.

I take a look at the digital information screen on the wall, seeing that the next line of train carriages will arrive in seven minutes time. A few other people stand around on the platform, waiting with me. Some read newspapers while others speak with colleagues or friends. There are only a handful like me, alone and quiet with their own thoughts. More guards patrol the area - the ever present force of security - and CCTV cameras are placed everywhere, watching all of us.

A speaker on the wall of the library sounds a dull siren in monotone bursts, each lasting for a couple of seconds. It is a signal from Central Government, a mandatory calling: an important message is about to be broadcast. Along with all the other people, I turn to face the large television screen on the wall of the station platform behind us, as we have been taught to do. We behave like domesticated pets, acting with loyalty, facing our master.

The screen fades in from black and a man appears, sitting behind a desk, holding a printed report in his hands. I recognise him from previous security broadcasts that have played in the past. He looks very smart in a grey suit, and his hair is styled neatly with a central parting. He emits the appearance of a serious professional, a person I can trust completely. I'm smart enough to know this is a fabricated image, purposely created to reassure me and everyone else who is watching.

'Residents, I speak to you today about an important security matter. We have a male Rogue on the loose. He has been categorised as level three, which, as you all know, means there has been no previous history of violence, although he could easily develop an unstable attitude, or cause harm, if agitated by a situation.
Do not approach him.
If seen or encountered, contact your local Community Guard office.
Be safe, and know that your Government is here for you.
This threat will be eliminated.'

All the people on the platform sound and act shocked on hearing this news. They begin talking to each other in fast and broken sentences, gasping at the unexpected announcement.

I am also worried to hear about a criminal walking the streets where I live and a few thoughts darts across my mind. *Was he in there ... with me?! Did I see him without even realising? Has he been tampering with books?*

An understanding of my ordeal inside the library earlier this morning begins to unfold with the help - unneeded help - of my fear fuelled thoughts.

The criminal class of 'Rogue' is given to those questioning any laws, or spreading propaganda in an attempt to corrupt the behaviour of others. It could be as simple as whispering an idea to another resident, planting the first spark of distrust. I've even been told stories about deranged individuals, screaming lies as they run through the streets.

Rogues were initially categorized and considered dangerous by researchers from the Science Department of

Central Government. They discovered evidence which proved the unusual actions - often non-conformist in their nature - also indicated early symptoms of infection from the virus.

Stay calm. The Community Guards will deal with it! I think to myself, slightly easing my own fears.

An image appears on the television screen of a man in his mid-thirties. His brown eyes are menacing and bloodshot which makes me relieved that I don't recognise him from the photograph. His appearance scares me, sending a shiver up my spine as I imagine him walking through the library.

Familiar words flash across the screen: *'Central Government is always here for you.'*, followed by their instantly recognisable insignia, all in grey tones. Using various shapes and lines sat inside a square, it illustrates society, Central Government departments, security services, and the safety of the Community Zones. The outer square is always deemed as the most significant, especially by parents, teachers or Government officials, because it represents the perimeter, the border that keeps every resident safe inside. The methods used differ, depending on the community and geographical layout: an electrified fence, a thick wall built ten feet high, a deep trench or moat … my own community has a mine field. Many pressure activated explosives are buried under the soil, reaching for a quarter of a mile. The fifty-fifties or wild animals will never be able to enter here. *I've never seen any, though, or heard older people speak of them trying to.*

If they were to ever make it through, Community Guards are stationed close by with more automatic weapons and fire-power than I care to imagine.

The screen fades and a different message begins to play - smiling children and their equally content parents. After ten seconds it will change again to another similar one, or show a montage of Government officials with messages of inspiration typed underneath: *I am Minister Howle. I am in charge of the Department for Housing, always working to keep your home sterile, safe, and comfortable.*

With gentle vibrations in my feet and legs, plus a low hum, the train arrives and I step on, finding the nearest empty seat as quickly as possible. I still want, and need, to sit down after the Community Guards stopped me earlier. The journey will hopefully provide the perfect opportunity to compose myself before the progression interviews. *I'm already nervous, I don't need it to get worse ...*

A memory surfaces, caused by the train jolting forwards, replaying in my head as I stare out of the window at the buildings.

At the age of eleven, shortly after beginning my first year of senior education and career decision, all the children in my geography class were taken to one of the communities near the old city of London. History lessons have taught me that it was previously a bustling and highly populated city, prominent too - the capital of England up until the year the virus grabbed the world in its fatal grip. London is now the same as every other community, though, and holds no standing in the country. The power in the world doesn't have a residence. It moves around ... an unseen entity, following all those privileged enough to wield it.

Our class passed through a Wild Zone on that day. We were all fascinated to see the lush trees, acres of green grass and various flowers, yet filled with fear on seeing a pride of lions prowling through an open field. It was the first time any of us had seen such creatures first hand. They looked savage, dangerous, and majestic. In bewildering contrast, part of the old London could be seen from the safety of our train. The Science Department quarantined the area many years ago, finding it to be contaminated with pathogens and uninhabitable to those fortunate enough to live in the Community Zones.

I remember the dust and grey earth blowing in the

wind. It swept across empty roads and moss covered buildings. Some of them had become victims of time and weather erosion, crumbled to near ruin. I imagined a giant walking through the city, destroying buildings with every footstep.

Photographs and video recordings do exist and are still used for educational purposes, although they show nothing but the deserted streets - post virus devastation at its most basic level. Tall buildings, vast road networks, monuments built to praise people of historical significance … yet, because there are no people in those images, there is no life. The whole story can't be told or imagined with any detail … with any heartbeat.

The innocent recollections fade away to the back of my mind as the reality of my location takes over - the Essex Community Jurisdiction Bureau looms only minutes ahead. The size of the building always intimidates those who see it or visit here, and Central Government are known to renovate regularly, adding more extensions in thick concrete. Build … stack … repeat.

The exact dimensions or number of staff are unknown to me, yet I do remember from leaflets sent out to schools that it is approximately a mile wide. A whole mile of concrete domain, sitting high above everything else. It is placed centrally in the community, with a barracks containing Community Guard housing, plus armed forces as well, surrounding the complex. Air defence hangars contain fighter jets and helicopters, ensuring that every location in the zone can be reached within forty-five minutes. All situations, trivial or major, are dealt with swiftly and safely. As I am often told by those in power: *The normality of life has to be maintained.*

The Bureau building always reminds me of the housing estates that I know so well, although it is an amplified, exaggerated version of them. From birth to the age

11

of eleven, I lived in one myself. I was the proud and content occupant of living unit 903, 9th floor, South Quarter.
Once my father achieved a promotion, he also earned relocation privileges, meaning we were then permitted one-level living quarters. It resembles the design of the estate unit, yet is much larger inside, with more hours of rationed water included.

The train slows down as the large station appears. It looks completely different to all the others I have used in my life. They are mundane and purposeful, nothing else, yet this demonstrates why career progression, status, and reward for serving Central Government are values in life to aim for. In full view, for all to see, coloured kiosks are built on the platform, allowing fruit flavoured juices to staff members of particular grades, plus, these extras won't be deducted from their weekly food rations either. There are also delicacies that I've only heard of: peanut butter sandwiches, plain sponge cake, decaffeinated coffee.
I always remember an important Central Government ideal when I see or think of this place:

'Aspire to serve your Government. Be a person of virtue, of understanding, of loyalty. Work hard and you could be rewarded.'

The train stops and the doors open. I politely let a woman step out first - I am in no rush whatsoever to begin these interviews because anxiety is controlling me now. I take in a large gulp of calming air, then step off the carriage.

••

The main lobby of the Jurisdiction Bureau surrounds me like a huge concrete hand. I'm barely allowed a second in time to take in the vast space before an assistant in a light-grey tunic approaches. He taps at the screen of the digital pad which he is holding, then looks at me with what seems to be impatience.

"Follow me, Elana, I'll escort you to the interview," says the young man as he turns his attention back to the display. He is in his mid-twenties with short blond hair and green eyes. The abrupt nature of his words and body language put me on edge.

"Thank you," I reply. I am instructed immediately afterwards - with nothing more than a few waves of his hand - to hand over my ID card.

"This way," he says as the digital pad scans my card.

I don't even know his name. He could have at least introduced himself. He knows how intimidating this place is ... especially today!

After being escorted through the building for ten silent minutes, along many corridors - all that seem to have no end - I finally reach a small room.

Without a hint of manners or politeness, I am directed to wait inside until a representative of the Education Department calls for me.

On the wall opposite my chair, a television screen replays the warning message that I watched earlier at the college library train station, with an update added to the end - the Rogue male still hasn't been apprehended. Apart from that, there isn't anything else to look at. No photographs have been placed on the walls showing content families, smiling at each other.

"Elana Mayne."

The female voice comes from a speaker somewhere in the room, although it is completely hidden from view.

"You may now proceed to your interview. Leave this room, turn left, enter the first door on your right. Introduce yourself, then wait for further instruction."

I stand up and shake my arms and hands with vigour and too much strength. They feel hot and overly sensitive, as if pins and needles are trying to set in. *Here we go!* I think, encouraging myself to be successful.

I follow the directions and soon find myself in a large and windowless hall. Thick panels of transparent plastic separate it in equal sections, and a couple of chairs have been set out, facing each other. They seem too close. Intimidating. *Do I sit? I haven't been told to ...*

I immediately notice others there too, all looking as nervous as I do, all standing by the chairs, wondering who might soon sit in them. *This is it. I wonder if it really is as bad as I've heard?*

Loud clicking noises from the heels on a pair of shoes sound behind me as a woman walks in through the same door I used: late-forties in age, her hair is tied up in a neat style, and she has serious hazel eyes. She wears a beautiful red dress and matching shoes, making me wish that I owned such clothes.

As the woman stops, I speak straight away. "My name is Elana Mayne. I reside in the South Quarter of the Essex Community." My words are rushed yet coherent.

The woman doesn't respond because she is too focused on reading through a file in her hands. I have a terrible feeling she is scouring my personal information for a reason to complain ... something, *anything,* to pick up on.

The wait makes me even more nervous, yet I manage to hold myself together. I am the prey ... and she is a coiled snake. At any moment she will lunge forward, striking with venomous fangs.

Breathe ... breathe ...

"Let us begin," she says. Her face is very sharp - every chance it has to point, it does: her chin, her eyebrows, even the corners of her mouth. She is created from angled stone. "I see you've presented yourself well today. Always a good start."

"Thank you ...," I fumble at my words and panic, realising I am unsure how to address this woman correctly. Is it Professor? Minister? How have I overlooked such a fundamental part of this day? "… ma'am," I say after an awkward length of time.

"You may call me *Miss* Collins."

"Thank you, Miss Collins," I add with an apologetic smile. I doubt it will help.

"I have no concerns about your academic record, Elana, so some of the departments won't need to see you today. Perhaps a little bit more of an effort could have been shown in some of your weaker subjects, though …," says Miss Collins with a few taps of her pen. "… but I won't hold that against you. Others might."

Weaker subjects? I'm slightly confused and thrown off my guard by those two words. I honestly wasn't aware I had any because all of my current grades are eighty-five percent or above. I flick a nervous glance around the hall, seeing all the others in here are now being greeted in a similar fashion. A tall and muscular man, late forties as well, stands in the section to my right, talking to a boy I recognise from college … *Good luck, Andrew.*

"Yes … adequate … I see no real problems here … apart from distraction. Are you easily distracted, Elana?"

"No, Miss Collins. I'm only taking in my surroundings … and the situation." I cough the last part of my sentence. My voice has turned a little croaky because my mouth feels dry. "Interviews, especially one as important as this, will no doubt make everyone nervous."

"No, Elana, they won't. I am not nervous, not in the slightest bit." Miss Collins raises an eyebrow. Her eyes widen and her lips scrunch together with disapproving tightness.

The hunter isn't scared of the prey …

"Kindly keep your eyes on me and ignore your surroundings. Now, tell me, Elana, which department interests you? Where do you see your career path heading?"

Her eyes look up and grab me in a stare that will not

let go.

"Any of the sciences, Miss Collins. They interest me a great deal and are my strongest subjects, as my grades show. I enjoy studying them at college … I always have. I believe I will be able to serve Central Government in that field, if they choose to further my training, of course."

"The sciences?" asks Miss Collins. She looks and sounds a little disappointed with the answer and her hazel-eyed stare grows in strength, drilling beyond my eyes. Her body doesn't move, as if she isn't even breathing.

"Yes …" I desperately want to add something else, yet I also don't want to repeat my first statement. I'm trapped in silence by hesitation.

"So, not able to provide me with a specific answer? A little bit of indecision as well. What a shame. I shall have to make a note of that." Miss Collins scribbles in the file as she speaks to herself. "… indecisive attitude … distracted …"

Again, I feel the urge to add more, yet now it will seem as if I'm doing it for all the wrong reasons: trying to impress Miss Collins, or changing my answers because I have been prompted to. I admit to myself with a sigh and the threat of tears that this interview … the *interrogation* … has not begun well for me.

"And … this surprises me a great deal, Elana, a great deal …" Miss Collins pauses as she flips over pages in her file, scanning the print with excruciating precision. "… I can't find any incidents in your records where you have felt the need to speak to the Community Guards. We've all seen crimes or indiscretions in our lives, all of us. Why haven't you ever reported any?"

My mind empties. It is completely blank and no answer appears.

"… inability to form suitable replies … possible willingness to ignore fundamental law …," says Miss Collins as she scribbles once more, then locks me in her unnerving glare. "Trust me, though, Elana, that soon fades with the onset of adulthood … and the responsibility that accompanies it."

I simply nod, wanting her eyes away from me.

••

The next hour continues in a similar fashion. Various representatives move about and through the sections, each with their own brand of questions and demeanour. The man I'd seen to my right when I first entered is here on behalf of the military - Commander Ward. His uniform has three black CG insignia placed on both the shoulders of his thick green jacket, indicating rank and which department he works for. Just to ensure I felt clouded by rudeness for the whole day, he never even took the time to introduce himself.

Within ten seconds of our encounter, Commander Ward looked at my average body size with frustration, measured my five-and-a-half feet height with a digital scanner, then, with a bored look on his face and a loud sigh, asked me to tense '*whatever biceps I might have*'.

After doing so, he rudely walked off without another word, immediately deciding I wasn't worth interviewing at all.

When Miss Collins returns she is still impossible to read, still angled and made of sharp stone. Her unashamed mannerisms tell me that she is rarely impressed, or ever genuinely pleased with results.

Does she have to act like this? Is this her natural personality, or is it part of her career description to be so searching, so unpleasant?

"I shall forward your details to all the relevant departments, Elana. You will be notified of the outcome on the fourteenth of July. You may leave now."

Finally, I think with a hidden breath of relief, *it's*

over!

"Thank you, Miss Collins," I say and head towards the door. I notice the scared faces of all the others still being interviewed as I politely walk out of the hall, eager to escape this concrete fortress and see the outside world again.

••

With the Jurisdiction Bureau looming behind me, I somehow manage to relax myself, yet I can't gauge if I have failed miserably or managed to impress any of the representatives at all.

"I'm sure it will be fine … won't it? Miss Collins said that my grades were adequate … she saw no problems … I should have chosen a specific area of study, though … but … but that can't be too bad, can it?"

I mumble more retrospective conversations to myself while waiting for the train to arrive. I had been expecting a lot more involvement in the proceedings … a chance to prove myself with some intellectual or practical tasks. Not an hour standing in a room being questioned. *Why bring in chairs if we weren't even allowed to sit on them?*

Complete and utter embarrassment hits me as I remember more details, making my face glow hot and red. Commander Ward so easily dismissed me as a viable investment choice for further training because of my size and apparent weakness. Yes, I agree completely with his decision - I'm definitely not cut out for the military. I often make the same face as he did: usually when my mother cooks a thick, and not particularly appetising, fish stew.

The train arrives so I get up and walk towards an open door on one of the carriages. Then, something happens - something so quick and unexpected, my mind doesn't even have a chance to comprehend or explain it. One second my eyes are looking at the train, the next I'm laying face down on the floor. The entire front of my body aches because of the fall, especially my left hand. It feels warm as sharp pains shoot through my fingers.

"You must ask yourself ... How could I know any of this? Unless ...?" says a woman's voice, although it isn't familiar to me. It's very soft and delicate, as if spoken in a breeze.

I try to turn my face so that I can look behind me but the pain, confusion, and shock are all still too fresh.

"What ... what happened? Did I trip over? Was I pushed?"

Other voices grow louder as they arrive near to me, also wondering why I'm face down on the platform.

"I didn't see anything!" says a male voice. "Did anyone?"

"I think she's hurt herself!" says another - a young man.

"Come on, child. Up you get ... it will be fine. Sit for me so that I can check you over," says a different woman with a broader, mature tone. "Are you hurt?"

I have to force myself to think about the answer as I hear the sound of the train moving away. Most of the pain has lessened, except for my hand. "I ... I think so. My hand really hurts ... and my fingers ... they're stinging ...," I say

"I'll take you to a medical booth, child. Come on. Your fingers look swollen and need to be examined. Just hold them still for me, as best as you can. Don't move them ..."

I try to piece together the last minute. I want to remember what happened to me, what caused me to fall, but the only thing pushing to the forefront of my mind are the words of the unknown and unseen woman. *Who spoke to me? What did they mean?*

As I look about, I completely forget the mature woman's advice - because my thoughts are elsewhere - and push down on the floor as I try to stand up. A chilling howl of

pain leaves my throat as I grab the woman's hand in agony,
then roll back to the ground in tears.